APPOINTMENT ON THE YELLOWSTONE

Bliss Lomax was a pseudonym for **Harry Sinclair Drago**, born in 1888 in Toledo, Ohio. Drago quit Toledo University to become a reporter for the Toledo *Bee*. He later turned to writing fiction with *Suzanna: A Romance Of Early California*, published by Macauley in 1922. In 1927 he was in Hollywood, writing screenplays for Tom Mix and Buck Jones. In 1932 he went East, settling in White Plains, New York, where he concentrated on writing Western fiction for the magazine market, above all for Street & Smith's *Western Story Magazine*, to which he had contributed fiction as early as 1922. Many of his novels, written under the pseudonyms Bliss Lomax and Will Ermine, were serialised prior to book publication in magazines. Some of the best of these were also made into films. The Bliss Lomax titles *Colt Comrades* (Doubleday, Doran, 1939) and *The Leather Burners* (Doubleday, Doran, 1940) were filmed as superior entries in the Hopalong Cassidy series with William Boyd, *Colt Comrades* (United Artists, 1943) and *Leather Burners* (United Artists, 1943). At his best Drago wrote Western stories that are tightly plotted with engaging characters, and often it is suspense that comprises their pulse and dramatic pacing.

APPOINTMENT ON THE YELLOWSTONE

Bliss Lomax

GUNSMOKE

First published in the UK by Collins

This hardback edition 2011
by AudioGO Ltd
by arrangement with
Golden West Literary Agency

ISBN 978 1 445 85650 6

British Library Cataloguing in Publication Data available.

Printed and bound in Great Britain by
MPG Books Group Limited

1

The taller of the two men seated together in the smoking car fought the sticking window and got it closed. They had had it up and down all day.

"The cinders and dust are worse than the smells in this car," his companion said, with an approving nod. "They must have been puttin' in some new track along here, Pierce."

"They've been doing something," Pierce Hamlin agreed unhappily.

Both were travel-weary. A week and a day had passed since they left Denton County, Texas. It had been a succession of slow, comfortless trains and bad connections. Since early morning this three-car Northern Pacific local had been trundling across the monotonous miles of North Dakota's undulating plains.

There were a dozen or more fellow travelers in the smoker. Who they were and where they were going did not interest Hamlin. Two or three had come all the way through from Bismarck; the others got on at one station and off at the next. The towns were far apart, ugly, unpainted, sun-bleached, depending for their existence on the wheat farmers, Swedes, Norwegians and Finns, that the railroad's Land Department had been bringing in.

"I'm going to stretch my legs, Skip," Hamlin said.

Getting to his feet, he took a turn up and down the aisle. He was in his early twenties, a man with a large frame and lean. Though his features were good, he had a rather plain face. His black hair was thick and bushy. But if there was anything to distinguish him it was the determined set of his mouth and his alert, searching gray eyes.

He returned to his seat. Skip Roberts gave him a glance.

"Feel better?"

"I'll last it out," the tall man answered, with a half-smile. "The conductor says we're running only about two hours late. If we don't get off the track, we'll be in Broken Rock some time this evening. I suppose you know that's Montana you're looking at now."

Skip Roberts turned to the window and looked out. After a long glance, he shook his head dubiously.

"I'll be damned if it ain't the same country I been lookin' at all day," he complained. "Just sage, sand and some bunch grass. I don't see no cattle."

"You will later on, when we hit the Yellowstone."

Hamlin had been in Texas long enough to have acquired a slight Texas drawl, but when he spoke of the Yellowstone, he was speaking of his home country. Roberts was all Texan, and for the past two years had been riding top hand for the tall man's Denton County spread that had recently been sold to the Texas and Pacific at a fancy price.

He knew what was bringing Hamlin back to the Yellowstone, and more particularly to Yellowstone Basin, after an absence of five years. It wasn't money, or a girl's pretty face; he was coming home to square a debt—an obligation that for all those years he had gone to bed with and got up with and had never been out of his mind. Roberts knew trouble would come of it, serious trouble. He couldn't have said why he was letting himself be drawn into it; it wasn't his quarrel. As a matter of fact, though he was not aware of it, Pierce Hamlin had won such loyalty from him as he had never expected to give any man, and he was with him because he couldn't help himself.

Late in the afternoon the country began to look familiar to Hamlin. The train crossed a creek that he was sure was Black Tail and another that he knew was Ten Mile. The Basin lay to the south of the railroad and couldn't be seen, but Black Tail and Ten Mile headed there, and with little Squaw and Box Elder Creek supplied the water that made it the best grazing country in eastern Montana.

Old memories rushed back to him, most of them bitter. He recalled the evening, now a little more than five years gone, when he left Jeptha Tark's T Bar ranch and this Yellowstone country to begin the wandering that had taken him to Texas. The T Bar was then, as he knew it was now, the biggest outfit in Sioux Basin. Jep Tark, ruthless, cruel and ignorant, had made it big by fraud and trickery, or worse. Oftener than not, men who dared to oppose him soon found themselves being ground down under his iron heel.

When he was only a lad of ten, Pierce Hamlin's widowed mother married Jeptha Tark. He had hated the man from that moment to this, and not so much because of the beatings and abuse that had been his lot—though he hated him for that too—but for the misery and shame Jep Tark had heaped on his mother. Even as a boy he swore that the day would come when he would square his score against the bearded tyrant and his mother's as well. He had grown big and strong. At seventeen, he was doing a man's work on the ranch. He had not forgotten the promise he had made himself as a young lad. Time only burned it deeper into his consciousness, for Jep Tark's meanness increased as he became more and more prosperous.

On the evening Hamlin recalled so clearly, his step-father had returned from Broken Rock, half drunk. When he stalked into the kitchen and failed to find his supper waiting for him, he began to slam things around. "Damn you, Lottie, I want my supper on the table when I git home!" he bellowed. "You don't have to cook for the crew, jest me and Pierce. Looks like that's too much for you. I'll hurry you up!" He raised his hand to cuff her.

That was when it happened. Hamlin leaped in between them and drove his fist into Jep's face. Though it caught the latter by surprise and rocked him to his heels, he righted himself after taking a backward step. "So you figger you're big enough to stand up to me, eh?" he snarled. "Step outside! I'll take care of you!"

Though he was past fifty and had grown stocky with the years, he was as tough and hearty as an old oak. It did not take the boy long to discover that he was no match for the man. Jep cut him down as methodically as though he were felling a tree, and when he had battered him into unconsciousness, he doused him with a bucket of cold water and left him lying in the dust. His mother came to his room that night and found him gathering up his few belongings. He knew he had to go; that he would kill Jep if he didn't. He begged his mother to go with him. She had a few dollars for him, the pitiful savings of years. Jep had a woman in town, Annette Davis. It was an open secret. He had met her in a Miles City honky-tonk and brought her back and established her in Broken Rock. He squandered money on her, but never a cent on Lottie Tark.

"Don't try to write me, Pierce. He'd see that I never

got your letters; you see Lin Bible before you leave town. Keep in touch with him; he'll manage to let me know where you are and how you're makin' out."

Pierce Hamlin remembered his brave parting words; his renewed promise that he would be back some day and make Jep Tark pay for his cruelty and neglect and all the misery she had been forced to endure. Well, he was back now. It had taken longer than he had expected. Much longer. His mother had been dead for two years; he knew Jep Tark had put her in her grave with his brutality and neglect.

"I didn't want to come back penniless," he said, as he sat in the sheriff's office with Lin Bible the next morning. "I've got money, Lin, and I'm prepared to spend every dollar of it to pull him down."

"I don't know how you're goin' to go about it, Pierce. It'll take more than money—unless you've come back with the idea of gunnin' him down at the first opportunity."

"No, I'm not interested in killing him. That would be too quick. I want to chop him down a little at a time and make him suffer the way he made my mother suffer."

The sheriff nodded in a way that was full of understanding. His hair and mustache had turned white in the years Hamlin had been away, but his unlined face was still ruddy as ever.

"I don't have to tell you, Pierce, how I felt about Lottie. After your pa died, I asked her to marry me. I don't know what she saw in Jep Tark in those days, but she chose him instead of me. I never let it make any difference; I went right on lovin' her. I know the dog's life he led her. In my way, I hate him as much as you do."

The old man broke off and his face grew sober as he sat there communing with himself.

"You want to watch yourself, Pierce," he said, looking up under his hooded brows. "When Jep hears you've come home, he'll know what brought you back. He's got upwards of fifteen men on the T Bar today, men he's brought in from outside who'll do his biddin', no matter what. You'll be gittin' out into the basin, I know. You keep this man you brought up from Texas close to you."

Hamlin accepted the advice in the spirit in which it was offered.

"I know that's not your way of telling me it was a mistake for me to come back. I've had this in front of me every day for years; it's been like having an appointment with destiny, Lin. Whatever comes of it, I'm going through with it. Just what is the situation out in the basin today?"

"As I wrote you, Jep's hoggin' everythin' he can git his hands on. His T Bar spread is a big outfit now. He's got a new foreman since your time. As for the little fellas, they're bein' forced out. There's a new man on the old Drew Oliver place; Drew couldn't stick it out no longer."

"What about Tom Lockhart?"

"He's havin' a tough time of it too. I remember when his Cross Keys cattle ranged as far east as the Squaw. No more; his Black Tail range is all he has left. Tom's still got a lot of fight in him. I figger he's the strongest man in the basin, but he ain't strong enough to stand up to Tark by himself. I don't know what your plans are, Pierce, but if I was you I'd see Tom Lockhart and Frank Adams and try to show 'em how dang foolish they are, goin' on this way, every man for himself, makin' it easy for Jep to gobble 'em up, one after another. Their only chance is to organize."

"That's fine when it works," Hamlin replied without enthusiasm. "I know from experience how hard it is to get a bunch of cowmen to forget their private squabbling and pull together. I went through that in Texas." He shook his head skeptically. "You can't do anything without a leader, Lin."

"Wal," the sheriff grunted, pushing back from his battered desk and giving him a long, thoughtful glance, "you're young, Pierce, but you could be the man they need. God knows they're well acquainted with your score against Jep Tark. There won't be no question about which side of the fence you're on. When you left Broken Rock years ago, you knew he was hated. It wasn't a patch compared to the feelin' against him today. When he took that Davis woman out to T Bar and turned the house over to her before your mother was cold in her grave, that was the last straw."

"You wrote me that he married her—"

"He did, a couple of months later. If he figgered he could square himself by marryin' Annette, he was mistaken. Of course all she's after is the old fool's money. Most folks will tell you they hope she gets it. I don't believe she will; Jep ain't that soft over her."

The sheriff glanced at his watch.

"If you want to walk out to the cemetery, Pierce, we better git goin'. It's after nine and I'm due at the courthouse in an hour."

The men and women they passed on the street gave Lin Bible a friendly greeting and had an impersonal nod for his companion. Several looked back, wondering if they should have recognized the tall man striding along with the sheriff.

"You look familiar, Pierce, but they can't place

you," the latter remarked. "You'll find them friendly to you; no one's goin' to hold it against you that you're Jep Tark's stepson."

They reached the dusty, neglected cemetery and he opened the sagging gate.

"It's a shame the way the town lets this place go," he declared apologetically, as he led the way down a weed-grown path to Lottie Tark's grave. Some of the headstones had fallen; others were leaning precariously. "I try to git out once a month or so and keep your mother's grave clean. I figger that's the least I can do." They turned to the left a few steps and he said, "This is it, Pierce."

Uncovered, they stood there in silence for a few minutes. Hamlin dropped to one knee and breathed a silent prayer. He had not only loved his mother but the very wretchedness of their lives had forged an added bond between them. He read the inscription on the neat little headstone.

"That surprises me, Lin," he said softly. "I didn't think Jep Tark would be decent enough to have a stone placed on her grave."

"As a matter of fact, he didn't. Me and some of Lottie's friends got together and put it there. There's memories here for both of us, boy, but we've paid our respects; we better go back now."

He took Hamlin's arm and led him away. They had left the cemetery and were walking along the dirt road when a man and a young woman in a buckboard came up behind them. The driver pulled his team to a stop on recognizing the sheriff.

"Lin, I'll give you a ride into town if you want to hop in in back. Mebbe one of you could crowd in on the seat—" He checked himself and gave Hamlin a scrutinizing glance. "Who's this young fella you got with you, Lin?"

Lin Bible chuckled. "I wouldn't expect you to recognize him, Tom. Mebbe Miss Carla would. She used to go to school with him."

"Of course I do!" the young woman exclaimed, pleasantly excited. "You're Pierce Hamlin! I don't suppose you remember me."

"I'd never forgive myself if I didn't," he laughed. "You're Carla Lockhart. And don't remind me that I spilled lemonade all over your new dress at the party at the Black Tail schoolhouse."

Carla laughed. "I wouldn't remind you, but I haven't forgotten. Do you know I still have that dress, Pierce? I couldn't begin to get into it today, but I've never thrown it away. It was my first party dress. When did you get back?"

"Just last evening." As a boy, he had never thought her very pretty, but he found her lovely enough this morning.

"You must come out and see us," Carla urged. "I'd love to have a long talk with you. Mother will be glad to see you too. She always thought you were such a gentlemanly boy. Of course," she added with a mischievous smile, "she didn't know you as well as I."

"Let me git a word in here," said Lockhart. "I want to ask you, Pierce, do you think it's safe for you to come back to this country?"

The soberness with which the question was asked rubbed the smile off Hamlin's face.

"I don't suppose it is," was his equally grave answer. "But I've had a lot of time to think it over, Tom. I'm sure you'll agree that I had to come back."

"I suppose so. But you're comin' back at a bad time,

I'm tellin' you. Things were never worse in the basin."

"He knows," the sheriff spoke up. "I had a long talk with him this mornin' and sorta filled him in. I advised him the first thing to do was see you. I want him to talk things over with you, Tom."

"Wal, if he has anythin' to say to me it certainly concerns Jep Tark." Lockhart scowled as he spoke and turned to Hamlin. "We better not git our heads together here in town, Pierce. You come out to the ranch tomorrow. I'll be expectin' you. If you fellas don't want a lift, we'll drive on."

Carla waved a parting hand. Hamlin and the sheriff waited for the dust to settle before they went on.

"That was luck, meetin' up with Tom like that," Lin Bible observed. Hamlin wasn't listening.

"Carla has sure changed some," he mused aloud. "She's a mighty pretty girl."

"I suppose that's what a young buck like you would notice," the old man snorted sarcastically. "You better take another look. You'll find there's more to her than that. She's got as much fight in her as you have. Jep and a couple of his men was ridin' down Black Tail this spring and goin' to cut- acrost her ma's garden. Carla ran out with a rifle and told the old pirate she'd kill him if he didn't turn back. And she would have. When you have your talk with Tom, don't go behind her back to do it; she'll help you more'n she'll hurt you."

When Hamlin got back to the Yellowstone House, he found Skip Roberts waiting for him.

"How did things go this mornin'?" Skip inquired.

"I've been warned twice already that I'm likely to have a slug put in my back when I least expect it."

"Two warnin's already and the mornin' only half gone," the Texan drawled. Behind his grin he was deadly serious. "I reckon we better go up to the room and unpack our guns."

2

They spent the rest of the day looking over a number of horses before they found two that satisfied them. They had brought their riding gear up from Texas, and just to get the feel of being in the saddle again, they rode down the river for several miles. The Yellowstone was running almost at flood stage, unusual for late May. Every creek in the basin, and a dozen others, north and south, flowed into the river.

"They're not responsible for this high water," Hamlin informed Roberts. "This is the late spring runoff from the Powder and the Tongue and the mountain streams far to the west. Seems a shame to see it all going to waste in a country that'll be scraping the bottom of the barrel for water, come August."

"Montana's a young state," Skip reminded him. "It won't have any money to spend conservin' water for ten, fifteen years. The politicians'll pass the buck to the Federal government, but it ain't likely anythin' will come of that for a long time."

"That'd be my guess," Hamlin agreed. "In the meantime, you'll see some of the big outfits building their own—nothing elaborate, just rock and earth fill dams that'll hold back enough water to see them through till the fall rains come. If you've seen enough, we better head back to town if we want to get dinner."

The Yellowstone House was old (old for Montana) but the rooms were comfortable and the food good. Save for the few local businessmen who dined there regularly, Hamlin and Roberts had the dining room to themselves. Their table was beside a front window. As they sat there, a round little man with a saddle leather face passed. He saw them through the open window and gave them what seemed to be a grudging nod.

"He gave us a good lookin' over," Skip drawled. "You know him, Pierce?"

"Yeh, he's old Shep Henry, the town marshal. He's been wearing the badge as long as I can remember. He's never cut much ice; the law in this country is Lin Bible."

"Is the marshal for sale?"

"How would I know?" Hamlin replied, surprised at the question. "I was just a kid when I left here. Why do you ask?"

"There was nothin' friendly in the look he gave you. He may be your step-pa's man."

"That's nonsense! Why would Jep Tark bother with Shep Henry?"

"I suppose his crew hits town ever so often and raises a little hell. If he's got the marshal in his pocket, nobody gits tossed into the pokey."

"That could be," Hamlin admitted. "It doesn't concern me."

"It might," Skip persisted. "If that old bastard decided that the best way to git rid of you was to frame you for somethin' the marshal would come in handy."

The tall man refused to take it seriously. "I swear to God you're getting awfully scary. You better wait till the cards are dealt. Finish your coffee and we'll go out and sit on the porch."

The past five years had wrought very few changes

on Broken Rock's main street. Grassel and Kuhn's general store had acquired a new front and the old Hammond home had been remodeled to serve as business property and now housed McKnight's drug store. That was about the sum of the changes Hamlin could see. As a boy, he had seldom got to town. It was always a great occasion, long to be remembered by him. He smiled to himself as he recalled how important everything had seemed, how big the buildings and how tempting the cakes displayed in the window of Huffaker's bakery shop.

As he and Roberts sat on the porch a team, drawing a light buggy, passed the hotel at a brisk trot and turned into an empty space at the hitch-rack in front of the bank. Hamlin straightened up and his mouth tightened. The other caught it and surmised the truth.

"So that's Jep Tark!" he grunted, "and the straw blonde with the big front is his wife." His tone was as offensive as he could make it.

"Yeh," was Hamlin's tight-lipped answer, hatred boiling up in him at sight of the man.

Jep Tark was thin. There were other changes in him. His deeply lined face was as cruel as ever, but he was no longer the unkempt, dirty-looking character in sweat stained levis and battered Stetson that Hamlin remembered. He actually gave the impression that he took a bath once in a while. His beard was trimmed, his boots polished. It was quite a transformation. The young woman seated at his side was responsible for the change. There was no other explanation.

"What's the matter?" asked Skip as he caught Hamlin's unconscious gasp of surprise.

"I can't believe my eyes. He didn't used to give a damn how he looked. You'd have taken him for a ranch bum in his filthy rags. You'd have said he didn't have a dollar to his name."

"Goldilocks has been workin' on him. You know there's no fool like an old fool when he falls flat on his face for a dame. I bet that bug-eyed buzzard is in love with her."

"No, not love. He couldn't love anything."

"Then just call it a reasonable imitation. Look at him helpin' her down from the buggy! She's got him eatin' out of her hand. Your friend Bible is talkin' through his hat when he says she won't git her fingers on the old goat's money. You can be damned sure a good-lookin' babe like that ain't wastin' her time on him for anythin' else."

Annette Davis (or Annette Tark, to be more correct) was a buxom young woman, no longer a girl but still on the right side of thirty. She knew what the feeling of the town was about her; she had been snubbed and suffered the contempt of too many women in Broken Rock not to know. She met it with a brazen indifference. Her mocking smile and the taunting tilt at which she carried her head were doubly infuriating to her female detractors. But they were mannerisms she had acquired long before she came to the lower Yellowstone. She had a voluptuous figure and she dressed to show it off to advantage. Though she now had money to lavish on her personal adornment, her taste in clothes was so bad that she achieved only a cheap flashiness that reflected her honky-tonk background.

Lifting her skirts to keep them out of the dust, she crossed the street to Grassel and Kuhn's. Jep went into the bank. He was still inside when she came back with some packages. She placed them in the buggy and went up the street to continue her shopping. She was gone fifteen minutes or more and returned with more packages. She took her place in the rig and began to fidget as Jep kept her waiting. Hamlin and Roberts were watching her.

Half an hour passed.

"She's beginnin' to steam," Skip observed, obviously enjoying her perturbation. "The old man better be showin' up or she'll go after him. It's almost time for the bank to close."

Hamlin just nodded. He knew that Jep had been informed that he was back and had opened a bank account that morning. "That's all right," he reflected. "It'll give him something to think about."

Annette was getting out of the buggy when Tark came hurrying up. She was fighting mad. They couldn't hear what she was saying, but its tone was obvious.

"Givin' him hell," Skip chuckled.

Jep was angry—but not so much with her. Passersby were getting an earful. Hamlin expected him to silence Annette with a snarl—that had always been his way—instead, he tried to placate her. He flashed a beetling glance at the two men seated on the hotel porch, as he untied the team. Taking his seat in the buggy, he was about to pick up the reins, when an old woman, armed with a horsewhip, ran out between the teams and began to belabor him. Jep raised his arm to protect his face.

The old woman, in a frenzy, struck him again. He leaped out and tried to wrestle the whip away from her. He got hold of it and gave her a push that sent her reeling back. Hamlin leaped over the porch railing and caught her as she was falling.

A small crowd had gathered quickly. They were incensed, and they let Tark know it. Shep Henry, the town marshal, ran up.

"What's the matter with you, Shep, lettin' that crazy

old fool run loose?" Jep railed at him. "Lock her up!"

The marshal grabbed the woman roughly.

"You take it easy, Shep," Hamlin warned behind his teeth. "You may have to take your orders from Tark, but don't you start mauling an old woman."

Lin Bible pushed through the crowd, his white mustache bristling. "You heard him, Shep! Take your hand off Mary's arm. I'll git one of these ladies to take her home."

Several women stepped forward and took charge of the woman. The sheriff turned to Tark.

"I'll take that whip, Jep. You know Mary ain't responsible for what she does."

Tark passed the whip over without taking his eyes off Hamlin. His lined face was livid with rage as they faced each other.

"You had me fooled with your fancy clothes," Pierce said with withering contempt. "Beneath your rotten hide you haven't changed at all; you're still pushing women around."

"I'll make you sorry you ever came back to the Yellowstone to throw the past up to me!" Tark growled in a tone that was familiar to the other.

"I didn't come back just to dig up the past," said Hamlin, keeping his voice down but pouring into it all his vengeful determination. "I'm going to pull you down and drive you out of this country."

Jep Tark sucked in his breath noisily and glared at him in trembling, hate-ridden silence for several moments. He summed up what he was thinking in one brief sentence:

"You been warned, Pierce—"

"And so have you," the latter returned coolly.

Jep backed the team out into the street and drove

off. The sheriff walked back to the porch with Hamlin and Roberts.

"What was that all about, Lin?" the former asked. "The old woman, I mean—"

"You remember the Bibbs who used to own a little spread on Squaw Crick? They had a daughter about your age—"

"Mary Bibb—"

"Yeh! That old woman is Mary's mother. Folks call her Crazy Mary. She's a bit teched. She lives here in town with her son-in-law. You'll git used to seein' her around town with her horsewhip. The only time she makes any trouble is when she sees Jep Tark. She's gone after him four or five times."

"Why, Lin?"

"He kept crowdin' the Bibbs till they had nothin' left. Jim Bibb brooded over it for a couple of months, and then he rode out to T Bar one afternoon. Accordin' to the evidence at the inquest, he started throwin' lead at Jep. It was all over in a minute or two; a T Bar puncher killed him. It went down in the books as a justifiable homicide and that was the last of it. Old Mary ain't been right since."

Hamlin gazed at him incredulously after he had finished. "Lin, do you mean to tell me that wasn't enough to fire up the basin men to take some sort of action—not knowing which one of them might be next on Tark's list?"

"Oh, they had a secret meetin' and did a lot of talkin'. Somebody tipped Jep off to who was there. He rode around the basin for a couple of days with some of his crew, calling on those who had been present and threatenin' this one and that and warnin' whoever he was talkin' to that he'd make an example of him if he didn't mind his own business. That ended it."

"What's the matter with those fellas?" Skip demanded contemptuously. "Ain't they got no backbone?"

"They got plenty backbone, Roberts," the sheriff replied, testily, not liking what the Texan was implying. "They also got families and most of 'em are jest gittin' out of debt. They can't afford to lose the little they got. They ain't like the old-time free rangers, livin' out of a chuck wagon, with no responsibilities to anyone but themselves."

"I didn't mean to rub you the wrong way, Sheriff," said Skip. "A family man, with a wife and kids, has more to fight for than a single man. I figger nothin' should stop 'em from standin' up to that old range hog. As for losin' what they got, that's exactly what'll happen if they don't."

"I'm sure they'll fight if Pierce can show them how it's to be done and convince them that they got a reasonable chance of comin' out on top."

Hamlin and Roberts left Broken Rock soon after breakfast. They followed the main travelled road to the basin for a few miles and then turned off to climb the high bluffs to the west of Ten Mile Creek. An hour later, they had the basin spread out below. It was all as Hamlin remembered it. He pointed out the creeks and identified them for Skip—little Squaw Creek, Box Elder and Black Tail, which broke through the high Buckskin Hills to the south and flowed north across the basin to meet the Yellowstone, its winding course clearly indicated by the fringe of willows and occasional cottonwoods that grew along its banks.

"Those mountains to the east are the Buckskins," he explained. "Around the basin, when you speak of the Buckskin Hills you don't mean the Buckskin Mountains. Remember that, Skip. It'll throw you if you don't."

"It's beautiful country," Roberts declared admiringly. "Looks like Black Tail is the important water. I suppose Tark has grabbed most of it."

"So I understand. We'll follow the north rim around to Lockhart's place. It'll make us a little more riding, but I figure it will be safer."

Roberts speared him with a glance that was both sober and amused. "You figger Tark's sent out a man or two with orders to cut our trail and knock us off?"

"I do. He wouldn't hesitate a minute. We'll play it safe and give T Bar a wide berth today. You can't see the house from here, but we will when we swing a little further east."

They went on a quarter of a mile and pulled up again.

"There it is," Hamlin said, glancing far across the basin. "You can see the house just below where Black Tail comes out of the hills."

It was a big, box-like building, ugly even at that distance. The trees his mother had planted had either died or been cut down. Though he had been miserably unhappy there, sight of the old house had a nostalgic impact on him.

His thoughts were far away, when Roberts yelled:

"Look out, Pierce! Git down!"

Roberts was already out of the saddle. The sharp, flat crack of a rifle shattered the morning stillness before Hamlin could move. The slug screamed close as he flung himself to the ground.

Roberts had rolled behind a bank of loose rock. Hamlin crawled in beside him.

"Where did that shot come from, Skip?"

"From that ledge about two hundred years ahead of

us. Run your eye along it to where it notches. See the tip of his rifle?"

"Yeh—"

"I caught the sun glintin' on it just before I yelled." Roberts wiped the blood from his scratched chin. "I didn't waste no time gittin' in here. That bastard must have had orders to take no chances and git his turkey cold."

"We can't do much from here with a six-gun. You throw some lead at him, Skip, and keep him busy for a few minutes; I'll try to get around in back of him."

Roberts just nodded. The moment was not new to him; he knew the less talk there was, the better. He began firing. Hamlin crawled away. There were breaks in the cover he could find. Timing his advance with the bushwhacker's shooting, he crossed them without drawing a shot and began to swing around the ledge behind which the rifleman lay. It took him longer than a few minutes, but he was within a few yards of the man when he caught his first glimpse of him.

"I got you covered!" he called. "Throw away your gun!"

The other froze where he crouched and then slowly turned his head. When he saw that the jig was up, he flung his rifle aside and got to his feet with his hands raised.

Hamlin yelled to Roberts and told him to come on.

The bushwhacker glared at him defiantly and cursed him with a will. After searching him for a hidden gun and not finding one, Hamlin told him he could lower his hands. The latter, a little, thin, stoop-shouldered man, no longer young, with lines in his face that only hard work could have put there, continued to hurl abuse at him.

"Button your lip or I'll give you a pistol-whipping

you won't forget," Hamlin threatened. "You're old to be riding for T Bar and doing Tark's dirty work—"

"Stop right there, mister! I ain't seen you before, but you damn well know who I am and that I ain't wearin' that old buzzard's brand, and it's to yore shame that you can't say the same!"

Roberts came hurrying up with the horses. His face was lumpy with rage. "So this is the pup who tried to down us!" he whipped out thinly. "Why didn't you bust him, Pierce?"

He raised his hand to bring his gun down on the man's skull.

"Wait a minute, Skip!" Hamlin commanded. "There seems to be a mistake here. He claims he isn't a Tark man; he thinks we are."

"You believe that?"

"I don't know, Skip. It won't take me long to find out." Walking up to the man, he said, "I'm Pierce Hamlin, Jep Tark's stepson. I left this country years ago. Does the name mean anything to you?"

The other backed off and regarded him owlishly. "Yo're Lottie Tark's boy? You mean that?"

"I mean it. Who are you?"

"I'm Price Pickens. That's my ranch down below. Ever since the grass came green this spring, Tark's been doin' his damndest to push me back acrost the basin, stampedin' my stock so often I can't put no fat on 'em, pullin' down my fences. Twice in the last week he's had men up here beefin' some of my steers. I figgered I'd lay out up this way and throw some lead myself. I sure thought you was the gents I was lookin' for." He shook his head regretfully. "I'm sorry, I mistook you boys. God knows, Hamlin, you couldn't be lined up with Jep Tark after the way he treated yore ma and you."

"If there's any doubt in your mind about where I stand, it won't be there long," Hamlin informed him. He couldn't recollect having had any acquaintance with Price Pickens, but he remembered the name. "I know you're not the only outfit that's having trouble with Tark. Are your neighbors giving you any help?"

"Hell no! They got troubles of their own, son."

"Then you must be beginning to realize that you can't go it alone and beat him. He'll keep coming at you till he's got you where he wants you."

"That may be," Pickens conceded soberly. "But I'll tell you this, Hamlin, I'll go down fightin'!"

"If that's the way you feel it's good enough for me, Price. My friend Skip Roberts here and I are going around the basin for a talk with Tom Lockhart. Maybe you better come along with us. I'd like to have you sit in on it."

"Wal, I'll jest go you on that. I got my bronc hid back in the rocks."

Roberts had picked up Pickens' rifle. "You want to be careful how you use this thing," he admonished, as he handed it to him. "You won't help yourself none by knockin' off your friends. Some of those slugs came mighty close."

"Reckon so," Pickens declared, with a dry, cackling laugh. "I sure was shootin' at you, wasn't I?"

3

Tom Lockhart was one of the first stockmen to settle in Yellowstone Basin. He had prospered over the years and was well on his way to owning a sizable outfit until he ran afoul of Jep Tark. For a long time, he had employed a six-man crew. He had only three men riding for him now. His ranch still was, as it always had been, with its comfortable house, out-buildings in good repair, and its trees and garden, the prettiest place in the basin. Black Tail Creek swung around the ranch yard in a half-circle as it hurried on to the Yellowstone.

It took Skip Roberts' eye. "He's got everythin' here a man could want."

"You mean he did have till that high-binder across the basin began cuttin' into him," Price Pickens growled. "Tom will tell you."

They rode up to the house and Hamlin went to the door. Mrs. Lockhart, a plump, smiling little woman, came out.

"Why, Pierce!" she exclaimed, "it's so nice to see you again! What a fine, tall man you've grown to be. Lottie, bless her soul, would be proud of you."

She had a merry, chirping voice.

"I see you've got Price Pickens with you," she went on. She nodded to the latter. "I wasn't expectin' to see you, Price."

"No, I'm kinda here by accident, Miz Lockhart," Pickens answered with a grin. "They asked me to tag along and I figgered I might as well."

Hamlin made her acquainted with Roberts. "I brought him up from Texas with me, Mrs. Lockhart. He's a mighty handy man with a knife and fork," he added banteringly.

"I'm sure he could say better for you than that, Mr. Roberts," she laughed. "Pierce, Tom and Carla are down at the horse corral with Frank Adams, dickerin' about some broncs. You'll see them. You all will be stayin' for dinner, of course."

They went on. Carla waved when she saw them coming. Lockhart and Adams had just about completed their business. There was a difference of ten dollars between them on the two horses the latter wanted.

"All right, Frank," Lockhart told him, "I'll meet you halfway."

Adams agreed to it and the deal was closed. Hamlin remembered Frank Adams from Squaw Creek, and recalling what Lin Bible had said, he was pleased to find him there, so an introduction wasn't necessary. He made the two men and Carla acquainted with Roberts.

"I told Frank I was expectin' you, Pierce," said Tom. "He's interested in hearin' what you've got to say. Suppose we walk over to the barn and set down; the sun's a mite warm this mornin'."

He didn't exclude Carla from his invitation. She fell into step at Hamlin's side. There was something clean and wholesome about her that appealed to him. Looking down at her from his great height, he was more than a head taller than she, he remarked to himself that, for a girl who certainly spent as much time in the sun as she did, her skin was smooth and lovely and only faintly tanned. He understood that some women were that way.

"Frank Adams' opinions carry some weight in the basin, Pierce," she said for his ears alone. "I don't know what you're going to say, but if it's some plan for curbing Jeptha Tark, I hope you'll be able to convince Frank that it's worth trying."

"Sounds like you're on my side, Carla," he smiled.

Without looking up, she said: "I know something has to be done. We can't go on like this much longer."

Lockhart led them into the barn.

"We don't see you only once in a blue moon, Price. What brought you over this mornin'?"

"I had a little trouble with Pierce and his friend, up on the bluffs west of Ten Mile. There was some shootin'—considerable, I might say. I figgered they was a couple of the T Bar skunks who had been beefin' my steers; I'm damned if they didn't take me for a Tark hand. It took a little doin' to get things set straight."

Pickens' account of what had happened on the bluffs was complete enough to make it unnecessary for Hamlin to add anything. Lockhart expressed his opinion of the incident without mincing words.

"I suppose a man can git so desperate that bushwhackin' seems all right to him. But it's a bad business, Price. It was just luck you didn't kill a couple of innocent men."

"I know it, Tom, I know it!" Pickens agreed, throwing up his hands in his irritation at being criticised. "Of course, I coulda been killed too."

"You should have considered that before you squeezed the trigger," Frank Adams told him. He was blunt about it. "So far, we've kept our hands pretty clean in this trouble we're havin' with Tark. If we resort to bushwhackin', it'll give him all the excuse he needs to turn his wolves loose on us."

Lockhart nodded grimly. "It would be the worst mistake we could make. God knows we got strength enough in the basin to stop Tark cold if we only had the sense to throw in together and stand up to him."

That was obviously so true that Hamlin couldn't see how it was possible for the small outfits not to realize it. Lockhart's solution so closely paralleled what he himself had in mind that he waited anxiously to hear Adams' reaction to it. The latter was quick to say:

"I'd be the first to agree with you on that, Tom. But we tried it once, and nothin' came of it."

"Isn't it a fact that you stopped before you even got organized?" Hamlin queried.

"That's true, we had just the one meetin'. It was supposed to be secret, but somebody let word slip out and the next thing we knew Tark was ridin' the basin throwin' the fear of God into most of us."

"Frank, do you believe that was really what it was— just a slip—that supplied Tark with the names of those at the meeting?"

The question startled not only Adams but the Lockharts and Price Pickens as well. They turned on him as one. Hamlin's attention focused on Pickens. He couldn't be sure, but he thought the man flinched under his steady regard.

"I've never had reason to think otherwise than that somebody carelessly dropped a word," said Adams. His tone was less friendly. "You've been back only a day or so. You mean you know somethin' to the contrary about how Tark got his information?"

"No, I don't," Hamlin replied, "but ever since the sheriff talked it over with me yesterday morning, I've been asking myself why you men were so easily satisfied that it was just a little careless talk that got back to Tark. There were fourteen to fifteen of you present. He got the name of every one of you. Whoever supplied him with that information certainly knew what he was doing. It couldn't have been an accident."

"Pierce, you're bringin' up somethin' that Frank and I have discussed a good many times," said Lockhart. "We haven't ruled out the possibility that we've got a doublecrosser among us. If we have, he's covered himself mighty careful; we've never been able to turn up anythin' against anyone."

"It's very likely somebody who hasn't been hurt by T Bar," Hamlin pursued.

"That's right," Price Pickens declared vengefully. "That's the way to smoke him out. God knows it ain't one of us three; we been takin' it on the chin time after time. Go over the names of them that was at the meetin'. If we got a rat in the woodpile, that's the way to go about diggin' him out."

Lockhart and Adams shook their heads. "We've done that, Price, and it got us nowhere," the latter informed him.

"That's right," Lockhart agreed. "We accounted for every man who was here that afternoon. Every last one has had his share of trouble."

"Then mebbe Frank and you are all wrong about our havin' a traitor in our camp. I admit it looks queer, Tark gittin' all them names, but it don't prove we was sold out. It coulda happened some other way."

Hamlin was already vaguely suspicious of Pickens and this apparent readiness to have the matter forgotten tended to confirm what he was thinking.

"You made one mistake this morning, Price," he said pointedly. "Maybe you're making another." He was no longer sure that what had occurred on the Ten

Mile bluffs was the kind of mistake that the man had made it out to be. Without waiting for him to answer, he turned to Lockhart.

"Tom, you're giving everyone who attended the meeting a clean bill of health. Is that from hearsay or on your own personal observation?"

"I can account for most of 'em from personal observation." Lockhart recognized the merit of the question and was not irked by it. "Countin' my own spread, there's eight outfits strung along Black Tail. We've all been hit hard. I've seen it with my own eyes. Over on Ten Mile, there's Price here and Ben Southard. Ben's got about half the range left that he had a few years ago. Price has been whittled down to almost nothin'. Now I know those things to be a fact. Go over east to Frank's country on Squaw Crick . . . Frank, how many men you got ridin' for you today?"

"Just two—"

"And you used to have five, six. I reckon that tells its own story. You ride that country a lot. Up the crick from you there's Homer Knox and Dallas Wilcox. Is there any question in your mind about how they've been makin' out?"

"You know without askin'," Adams replied, with some annoyance. "The three of us visit back and forth, so of course I'd know what was goin' on. They can't keep a fence standin'. They been shot at a couple of times."

"Just bear with me, Frank," said Lockhart. "Pierce raised a point and I'm tryin' to answer him. . . . Now that leaves only young Wick Burnett, over on Box Elder—"

"You couldn't be suspicious of Wick," Carla spoke up immediately. "He's always been so ready to help.

No one is more outspoken against Jeptha Tark than he."

"I'll grant you all that," said her father, "and it may be that T Bar is makin' things tough for him; but I've got only his word for it. I got no reason to question it. Still, that ain't the same as knowin' he's been hurt. And that's the point I'm tryin' to make—sayin' what I know. I ain't been on Box Elder since last fall."

"I have, Dad, and not so long ago, if you'll remember." Some Lockhart horses had strayed and she and Buck Ross, one of the Lockhart punchers, had located them finally far up Box Elder Creek. "You have my word for it he's getting the same treatment we are."

With a stab of unconscious jealousy, Hamlin wondered if she had rushed to Wick Burnett's defense because of a romantic interest in the man.

"Who is Wick Burnett?" he asked Lockhart. "I don't seem to recall the name."

"You wouldn't, Pierce. He bought out Drew Oliver about three years ago. He seems to be a nice young fella, a couple years older than you. Hails from Kentucky originally. Tark's main push has been right down the middle of the basin; I wouldn't expect Burnett to git hurt too much, 'way over east on Box Elder." He glanced at Paula. "Did you and Buck talk to him?"

"We stopped at the house, but there wasn't anyone there. When Drew Oliver owned the ranch, he used to run his stock almost all the way into the mountains. T Bar cattle are on that range now. We saw one bunch within a mile of the house. A person has to believe his eyes, Dad."

"That appears to answer the point I raised," said Hamlin. "There's no need to pursue it further. If somebody is playin' Tark's game—and I'm still of that opinion—there's other ways of turning him up."

"Then mebbe we can hear what's on your mind," Adams suggested. "I can understand why you're anxious to git into this fight. Tom seems to feel you may be able to help us."

"If you are expecting me to pull some scheme out of the hat that'll turn the trick, you're going to be disappointed," Hamlin replied, addressing all of them. "As for helping you, that depends on whether you basin men can be pursuaded to help yourselves. Tark's pushing you around like a bunch of sheep, and he'll keep on doing it till he gets what he wants, unless you do as Tom says—organize, stand together and take the fight to Tark instead of waiting for him to hit you. It'll lead to gunsmoke. It'll be tough going. But that's part of the price you'll have to pay if he's to be stopped."

"Pierce, Frank and I and one or two others have considered takin' such a course," Lockhart informed him, his grizzled face hard and flat. "It means war, Pierce—all-out war."

"I'm afraid it does. But what alternative have you got? How much longer can you go on, with T Bar nibbling away at you a little today and a little more tomorrow? It won't be long before Tark has you gobbled up. It'll be just like eating a bunch of grapes for him. He'll pluck you off one at a time and when he gets through swallowing you you'll have nothing left."

"Yo're talkin' up a big storm, son—gunsmoke and all-out war," Price Pickens objected vehemently. "You jest wait a minute 'fore you say any more. I know it's in yore craw to git even with Jep Tark, and that's all right with me, but I'm damned if I'll go along with any scheme to use us to pull yore chestnuts out of the fire. We'd have to do the fightin', and we'd be in it up to our necks. You'd have nothin' to lose. If we didn't come out on top, you could say you was sorry. That's all there'd be to it."

Hamlin could see that the others found it a telling point. Addressing them all, he said frankly:

"There's some truth in what Price says. I'm glad he brought it up; I want to make my position clear. It's true that I want to pull Tark down. So do you. You know you've got to. You can help me. That doesn't mean it's my idea to use you; I want to get into this with you and see it through to the finish. I've got better than fifty thousand dollars on deposit in the Broken Rock Bank. I'm prepared to spend every dollar of it to win this fight."

Money and the power it represented impressed them, as it does most men. It had been their thought to listen to Hamlin and express a sympathetic interest and voice their mutual hatred of Jep Tark, but not to go beyond that. Though they had met with one reverse after another, and the pattern of what the future held for them was there to be seen, in their stubbornness they had been reluctant to admit that they were waging a losing battle. If he had accomplished nothing else, he had made them take a good look at what they had ahead of them.

A few minutes ago, they would have regarded it as preposterous that one so young as he could return to the basin, weld them together and lead them to victory. Now suddenly, they found it anything but far-fetched; he had the drive, the incentive and wherewithal to destroy Jep Tark.

A little chill, compounded of fear and pity, ran through Carla as she waited for him to continue. She knew vengeance was always cruel and bitter and that he was dedicated to it; that it was warping his mind. She pitied him for that and feared the excesses to which it might lead him. But she knew they needed him; that whatever it cost, his way was the only way left to them if they were to survive.

"I think it can be taken for granted that every one of you basin men owns some range," Hamlin resumed, undeterred by their silence, "but claim five to ten times as much under the provisions of the Customary Range Act. The act recognizes your right to use it, no more. You don't own the land. It can be sold out under you at any time—or you can be driven off it by any outfit strong and rich enough to make it stick. You can appeal to the courts, of course, but the courts don't decide in favor of the little fellow. You can put up fences on government land; Tark can knock them down and there's nothing you can do about it legally. That's his game; he isn't trespassing on the range you've got title to; all he wants is the free range you're using. When he gets done grabbing it, you'll have to take your cattle and pull out of the basin; you won't have grass enough left here to feed them."

It didn't come as a bombshell, but Tom Lockhart winced, recognizing its truth. Adams sat silent and immovable, his face rocky. Price Pickens just glared defiantly and chewed the ragged ends of his mustache.

"There's no point in goin' any further," Frank Adams said solemnly. "We can't decide anythin' this mornin'; the three of us can't speak for the others."

"That's right," Lockhart agreed. "I'm willin' to send out a call for everybody to be here tomorrow afternoon. I can git word around by then. There may be some who'll be afraid to come, rememberin' what happened the last time."

"If you make it clear that this is not to be another secret meeting; that we're through with going behind Tark's back to organize, they'll come," Hamlin said flatly. "Let his spy carry tales to him; that's exactly what we want. If we can't have a meeting on those terms, we better not have any. It would be meaningless."

Adams nodded approvingly. "I get your point. If a man hasn't guts enough to show Jep Tark by his presence that he is ready to stand up to him, then he's of no account to us. We'll know when we count noses tomorrow just how much chance we've got of makin' an all-out fight."

To Hamlin's surprise, Pickens expressed himself even more favorably. Wagging his head angrily, he said:

"Lay it right on the line to all parties concerned; make it a case of show up or shut up. That'll smoke 'em out. You don't have to bother about seein' Ben Southard; I'll be here and I guarantee you he will."

Carla excused herself and went to the house to help her mother. In a few minutes she called them to dinner.

Skip Roberts had been discreetly silent. Walking up to the house with Hamlin, he said: "You stirred them up, Pierce. I reckon you got a purty good idea already who the rat in the woodpile is?"

"Price Pickens?"

"Yeh—"

Hamlin shook his head dubiously. "I don't know what to make of him. But he'll bear watching."

The crew ate with the family. The conversation was general around the table. Mrs. Lockhart was famous for her cooking and hospitality. She made Hamlin and Roberts feel at home. She and Carla managed to keep the talk on the lighter side.

Hamlin sat at Carla's left. He found the friendly interest she expressed in him very pleasant. He spoke freely of the old days in the basin and his life in Texas.

"I'm glad you've come back, Pierce," she said. "I only wish it could have been under happier circumstances. As I listened to you this morning, I couldn't help feeling that we have great need of you. If you and your friend are going to spend some time in the basin, why not make your headquarters here? With our crew so cut down, there's room enough for you."

He was about to answer, when the sharp rattle of loose planks, as a rapidly-driven horse plunged across the ranch bridge, checked him. Through the open door, they saw the rider pull his mount to a slithering stop in the yard.

"It's Dallas Wilcox!" Carla exclaimed, getting up from the table. "By the looks of his horse, there must be something wrong."

Wilcox, a neighbor of Adams on Squaw Creek, hurried to the door. Lockhart told him to come in. The man, visibly distraught, focused his attention on Adams.

"Frank, I just came from your place. They told me you was over here. I wanted you to advise me what to do." He paused to gulp down a breath of air. "I've got myself into a hell of a mess!"

"What happened?" Adams and Tom Lockhart asked together.

Wilcox was one of the best-liked men in the basin. He was so shaken that he had to pull himself together before he could go on. Lockhart offered him a chair, but he refused it.

"My boy Ritchie shot a T Bar man this mornin'," he got out haltingly. "I can't tell you his name, but I seen him a number of times."

"Shot him?" Price Pickens burst out. "You mean he killed him?"

"Yeh—killed him. The body's layin' in the yard. I

threw a horse blanket over it before I left." His glance ran around the table without recognizing Hamlin. Roberts was a stranger to him, of course. "Good God, what am I goin' to do? As soon as he's missed, Strahorn will round up a bunch of men and come lookin' for him."

Joe Strahorn was the hated T Bar foreman, as dour and ruthless as the man whose orders he carried out to the letter.

With a little prodding, they got the story of what had happened out of Wilcox. The dead T Bar man had called him out of the house and given him just twenty-four hours to move his cattle off the Blue Flats, two thousand acres of good grass that Wilcox had been using for seven years. A heated argument had followed. Wilcox had ordered the man off the place. When he refused to go, and Wilcox ran to the house to arm himself, the T Bar man whipped out his gun. Ritchie, a lad of only fourteen, but big for his age and already doing a man's work, seeing what was about to happen, snatched up a rifle and killed the man.

Hamlin got to his feet and rapped on the table for attention.

"Now all of you listen to me," he commanded tensely. "That boy was within his rights; he thought his father was about to be shot down before his eyes. No jury in the country would see it any other way. But forget that for the moment. That T Bar man won't be missed until he fails to come in this evening. It'll be to-morrow morning before Strahorn starts out to look for him. That'll give us time enough to rock Tark to his heels."

"What's your idea?" Frank Adams demanded gruffly.

"Just this, Frank: we'll pick up that dead man, tie him on his horse and deliver him to Tark tonight with our compliments. We'll dump him right in the T Bar yard. That'll be doing something he'll understand."

4

The audacity of Hamlin's proposal held them in stunned silence for a moment. But it appealed to them.

"Why, I never!" Mrs. Lockhart cried, aghast. "Pierce, you certainly can't be serious, suggestin' anythin' as dangerous as that. If you're caught some of you will be killed—"

"Martha, this is somethin' that us men folks will have to decide for ourselves," Lockhart admonished her. "I'm sorry you had to hear it; I've always tried to keep such things away from you. I'm afraid that's no longer goin' to be possible." His attention shifted to Adams. "Frank, what do you think of this idea?"

"If we're going to fight, we couldn't find a better way to let Tark know it. We been waitin' for a chance to slap him in the face. I figger it would help Dallas. They'll be comin' at him, sure enough. We can't keep Strahorn from findin' out who killed his man."

"No, but we'll be letting T Bar know that some of us are standing by Dallas," said Hamlin. He glanced at Pickens. "What have you got to say, Price?"

"Oh, you can count on me; I'll be back here tonight. You don't want to start up the crick too early. Five or six of us will be enough; we don't need a big crowd."

With her eyes pinched with anxiety, Carla glanced down the table at her father, waiting for him to speak but knowing what his decision would be. He made it without equivocation.

"We'll leave here at nine o'clock. If we keep a mile or so to the east of Black Tail, we should be able to cross the basin without bein' seen. It'll be better if we're not."

"And in the meantime, nobody's to do any talkin'," Adams cautioned. "We ain't committin' no one but ourselves to what we're doin'. We'll be held responsible for what happens." He looked them over sternly. "Is that understood?"

They said it was. Lockhart suggested that they adjourn to the barn to complete their plans. "You sit to the table and have somethin' to eat," he told Wilcox. "Come down to the barn when you're finished. You give your mother a hand, Carla."

"We better not ask Wilcox to ride with us," Hamlin said, as they went down the yard. "He'll be worried about leaving his boy and the wife alone tonight."

He named the five; Lockhart, Adams, Pickens, Skip and himself. That was agreeable to them.

"It seems so foolish for you to make the long ride to Ten Mile and then have to turn around and come back, Price," Lockhart said to Pickens.

Hamlin was secretly interested in the need for it too.

"I'll have three or four hours at home," Pickens answered. "It'll give me time to see Southard and git him to promise to be on hand tomorrow."

It did not take them long to settle on the necessary details. Hamlin, Skip and Frank Adams were to go to Squaw Creek with Wilcox, with Adams continuing up the creek to inform Homer Knox of the meeting the next afternoon, and then cut across the basin to Wick Burnett's ranch on Box Elder to give him the message. Picking up the slain T Bar rider and bringing the body to Lockhart's was to be entrusted to Hamlin and Roberts.

"That leaves it to you to notify the men above you on Black Tail, Tom," said Hamlin. "That'll give you some riding."

"I'll take care of it," Lockhart assured him. "Here comes Dallas now. We might as well git ready to pull out."

"We'll let Frank and Wilcox show us the way," Hamlin told Skip, as the four of them crossed Black Tail and struck off to the southeast.

Presently they passed small bunches of Lockhart's cattle. Hamlin recognized the Cross Keys brand. Roberts, who never had too much to say, was singularly quiet.

"What's on your mind?" Hamlin asked.

"I'm wonderin' what we're goin' to run into tonight. Why didn't you object to havin' Pickens pull out to be gone all afternoon. If he's the informer, you can be damn sure they'll be expectin' us at T Bar."

"I thought of that, Skip. I figured if he's Tark's man the best way to find out would be to give him rope enough to hang himself. If we run into trouble, we can be sure it was he who tipped them off. Even though we may have to cut and run, it'll give Tark a jolt."

Roberts didn't like it. "I dunno," he drawled skeptically. "If they have a reception committee out waitin' for us, we'll likely git a considerable jolt ourselves. I'll grant you that if we've got a rotten apple in the barrel, we can't do much till we find it and throw it out; but gittin' our pants shot off will be a damned expensive way of goin' about it."

"We'll see," Hamlin responded with a touch of asperity. "We won't ride into anything blind; the two of us will go in a bit ahead of the rest; if they've got a trap set, we'll try to spring it."

The afternoon was half gone when they reached Dallas Wilcox's little spread on Squaw Creek. A glance at the dead man lying in the yard was all Frank Adams needed to make identification certain.

"It's Lem Dawson. He's been ridin' for T Bar a couple of years. Whenever Strahorn had a particularly nasty job to be done, Dawson always seemed to git the call."

"We won't shed any tears over him," Hamlin said unfeelingly. "What became of his bronc, Dallas?"

"It's in my corral—"

"You better get it. We'll roll this fellow up in the blanket and get him ready for the ride back."

Adams gave Skip and him a hand. When they had draped the dead man over his saddle and lashed him down, Hamlin called Adams aside.

"Frank, Wilcox says he's not going to move his stuff off the Blue Flats—"

"Good God, Pierce, are you goin' to advise that he should?" the other interjected hotly.

"Hardly! I figure it's up to us to see that he isn't pushed off. Dawson could have been killed any place in the basin; but Strahorn sent him on an errand, and you can be sure that he'll be coming here in the morning to ask how come. And he won't show up alone. Skip and I can be here about daylight. I'm sure Tom will send a man or two along with us. Can you get over here early with one or two of your men? That'll give Wilcox some backing."

Adams nodded. "I'll be here. We'll ride out on the flats with Dallas. Strahorn will understand why we're there."

"I'm sure he will," Hamlin said tightly. "It may cool him down some."

They acquainted Wilcox with the planned arrangement. Adams then continued on to Box Elder and Hamlin and Roberts turned back to the Cross Keys. Evening was coming on when they rode into the Lockhart yard. Out of consideration for Carla and her mother, they tethered the T Bar bronc and its grisly burden where the former would not see it. Carla came out on the covered gallery of the rambling house and sat down with them.

"Dad isn't back yet," she informed them. "He always likes to visit a bit."

"He knows we're not due to leave before nine," said Hamlin. "He'll be back in good time. Frank and I have agreed to be out on the Blue Flats with Dallas Wilcox in the morning, just in case T Bar tries to make him some more trouble."

He told her what the plan was. She gazed at him with a shrewd, unsmiling regard.

"Of course you realize, Pierce, that you're jumping the gun, with this business tonight and what you are going to do in the morning. You're not waiting for the meeting; you're going to present whoever comes with the accomplished fact that we're already at war with Jeptha Tark."

Her voice was steady enough, but he realized that beneath her surface calm her nerves were tense.

"That's one way of looking at it," he conceded. "It's my idea that if things go our way tonight and tomorrow morning, it may convince your friend Wick Burnett and the others that we can make out all right if we'll just quit acting like a bunch of scared rabbits and stand up to Tark."

His careless reference to Burnett as her friend was

unfortunate. Her chin went up and indignation drove the color out of her cheeks.

"I don't know that I've given you any reason to speak of Wick as *my* friend," said she. "I scarcely know the man."

"You spoke very highly of him this morning, Carla. I took it for granted that the two of you must be good friends. I'm sorry if I offended you. I'm sure you have many friends in the basin."

"I hope so," she said, somewhat mollified. "If I'm over-sensitive about Wick it's only because I know Dad doesn't like him. I can't tell you why, but I don't believe he really has anything against him except that Wick's a newcomer. I think you'll like him."

They were still talking, with Roberts saying only an occasional word, when they saw her father returning. She reached out impulsively and put her hand on Hamlin's arm. "Pierce, don't be foolhardy tonight. You'll have a hothead riding with you. Don't forget to keep an eye on him."

He knew to whom she referred. "You mean Pickens."

"Yes—"

"I'll be watching him," he assured her. If he was unduly emphatic about it, he had reasons of his own for keeping a close watch on the man.

Lockhart came up the gallery steps, slapping the dust from his shoulders.

"What kind of luck did you have, Tom?" Hamlin inquired.

"They'll be here. That was a sizable job, seein' all of 'em." Lockhart looked tired. He glanced at Carla. "Supper ready?"

"It will be, Dad, by the time you've cleaned up."

The sun was gone and the long summer twilight was spreading its magic over the basin and the distant Buckskins by the time they finished eating. Lockhart repaired to the gallery with Hamlin and Roberts and lit his pipe. They hadn't been there long when Frank Adams rode in.

"Are we all set?" the latter inquired.

"We'll have to wait for Price," Lockhart answered. "I expected he'd be here by now."

"I mean about the meetin', Tom."

"Yeh, they all said they'd be here. Alva Williams thinks it'll be a waste of time, but he said he'd show up. What did Burnett have to say?"

"He's comin'. It didn't take no urgin'. T Bar's sure got him whittled down; Carla was right about that. He sounds discouraged. Told me he wished he'd never left Miles City."

"He'll make out, I reckon," Lockhart said, his tone prejudiced. "He strikes me as the kind that always land on their feet no matter what happens."

An hour later, they were still waiting for Pickens. Lockhart had begun to fidget. Adams was visibly provoked. "What the hell ails him?" he grumbled. "He should have been here long ago!"

Hamlin and Roberts exchanged a poker-faced nod. There wasn't much doubt in their minds as to the reason for Price Pickens' tardiness. Hamlin said tersely:

"We'll give him another fifteen minutes. If he isn't here by then, we'll go without him."

They were walking to their horses, when the man from Ten Mile Creek jogged into the yard, unhurried and unapologetic.

"Why, what's eatin' you?" he protested irascibly, as Lockhart and Adams pitched into him. "I ain't late;

you said nine o'clock. I couldn't see no sense bustin' my neck to git here."

"Forget it, Price," Hamlin told him. "Let's be moving."

Looking back, as they left the yard, he saw Carla and her mother standing at one of the lighted kitchen windows, gazing after them. Their obvious anxiety was not lost on him.

They were far across the basin and on T Bar's home range before they pulled up to blow their horses and confer briefly. For the rest of the way, Hamlin was as familiar with the lay of the land as any of them, and more so with the T Bar yard itself.

"It's late," said he. "The ranch should be asleep, unless the old man and Strahorn have been tipped off. If they're expecting us, they'll be looking for us to come up the creek and move in from that direction. We'll fool them a bit; we'll make a wide swing around the house and reach the yard from the north. It will put the bunkhouse directly ahead of us. That'll be better than having it at our back. Of course, there's a chance that we may pull this off without a shot being fired."

"My foot!" Pickens snorted cynically. "Let's stop talkin' nonsense and decide what to do if they open up on us."

Hamlin regarded him with increased suspicion. "If we find them waiting, we'll have to drop back the way we came and use our guns to cover our retreat; we're not strong enough to fight our way across the yard and go hightailing it down the creek."

"That'll give 'em a damned good chance to cut us off before we git straightened out," Pickens objected. "We'd do better to bust right through 'em."

He looked to Lockhart and Adams for support, but they refused to go along with him.

"We'll do as Pierce says," Lockhart told him. "Let it go at that, Price."

Hamlin and Roberts went on ahead, with the T Bar bronc and its lifeless burden. The others followed, a hundred yards to the rear.

The scowl that furrowed Skip Roberts' face was an eloquent reflection of what he was thinking. "There can't be much doubt in your mind now about Pickens," he grumbled. "Sounded to me like he was tryin' to steer us into a trap."

"I'm afraid so, Skip. He may try to break away from us at the first sign of trouble. If he does, I'll stop him even if I have to drop him."

Presently they started swinging around the house. It was in darkness, and so was the bunkhouse. The night couldn't have been more peaceful. They looked back and saw the others following closely, before they entered the yard, walking their horses. It was only a minute's work to cut the ropes that held the dead puncher in place. They lowered the body to the ground and turned the horse loose.

All Hamlin's expectations of trouble appeared to have been unjustified. T Bar had been caught sound asleep. He didn't know what to make of it. He looked around for Pickens and caught him moving down the yard. He overtook him and pulled him up sharply.

"What are you up to, Price?" he whipped out angrily.

"That hay! Tark's got better than forty tons in the stack. I'm goin' to touch it off—"

"And start a series of hay fires all around the basin? You forget it! We're getting out of here now."

Their voices had risen. The bunkhouse door opened and a man ran out in his underwear. "Who are you?" he cried.

"It's Strahorn!" Pickens growled. He whipped up his gun to slap a shot at the T Bar foreman. Hamlin knocked his hand down.

"Stop it, you damned fool! You'll have the whole crew on us in half a minute!"

There was no one to stop Strahorn. He fired, and a smothered yelp of pain escaped the little man from Ten Mile. Men were pouring out of the bunkhouse. Hamlin caught Pickens' horse by the bridle and jerking the animal around, they raced out of the yard.

The T Bar guns were cracking in earnest now. Roberts and the others were answering the fire. A man stuck his head out of an upstairs window in the main house. It was Jeptha Tark. "What the hell's goin' on down there?" he screeched. "You, Strahorn, what is it?"

The basin men withdrew a few moments later and the night grew still again. As they moved down Black Tail, they weren't concerned about being pursued. They had caught T Bar unmounted. The folly of chasing them would be apparent to a man of Joe Strahorn's sagacity.

Hamlin drew up beside Pickens.

"Where did that slug get you, Price?"

"Jest clipped my ear. Bleedin' like hell, but I reckon it don't amount to nothin'." He was as belligerent as ever. "If you'd minded yore own business, I'd have got that bastard!"

"You're lucky to be alive," Hamlin rapped. "It was only a matter of an inch."

In another half an hour, Pickens turned off for home. It was one o'clock when the others reached the

Cross Keys. Lockhart had heartily approved Carla's suggestion that Hamlin and Roberts make the ranch their headquarters in the basin. They had accepted the proffered hospitality but only with the stipulation that if their stay was of any duration, they be permitted to pay for their keep.

"You better stay with us too, Frank, for the rest of the night," Lockhart urged. "You fellas will have to be back in the saddle by four if you're goin' to go out with Dallas in the early mornin'."

"All right," the other, agreed. "It's been a long day and we got another comin' up tomorrow."

Though both were pleased with the way things had gone tonight, and did not regret what they had done, they were restrained and taciturn, knowing only too well that there would be repercussions to the invasion of T Bar.

Carla and her mother were still up, waiting, when they rode in. They ran out and were relieved to have them back safe and unharmed. Hamlin and Skip took the horses and after stripping off the saddles and riding gear turned them into an empty corral. Roberts flipped a last smoke into shape and lighting a match, he waited for the sulphur fumes to burn off before applying the flame to the cigarette.

"Pierce, I wonder if we both have come to the same conclusion," the Texan drawled.

"I imagine we have, if you're referring to Pickens." Hamlin hooked a foot in the corral gate and indulged in a moment's sober reflection. "We were pretty much wrong about him. But not altogether. He's a mean, cantankerous, hotheaded troublemaker, but he's no Tark spy."

"I got to go along with you on that," said Roberts. "He had me fooled as bad as you. Bein' wrong about

Pickens doesn't mean somebody else hasn't sold out to Tark."

"You know it doesn't, Skip. Whoever he is, he'll be here tomorrow afternoon and I'll be looking for him. Pinch out that cigarette and we'll turn in."

5

Streaks of lemon and orange were already playing along the crest of the distant Buckskins when they moved out of the Cross Keys yard. Down in the basin, the blue-gray ground mist of departing night was beginning to rise.

They rode in a tight little knot, Hamlin, Roberts, Adams and two of Tom Lockhart's punchers. The sun put up its red face in a few minutes and quickly burned the moisture out of the air. Far off, a coyote climbed a point of rocks and bayed its obeisance to the God of Light. Adams dropped back a little until he rode beside Hamlin and got his attention.

"We may have Tark himself to deal with this mornin'. If not, Strahorn will sure show up. One or the other—it doesn't make any difference—he'll want to know who killed Len Dawson."

"It would be strange if he didn't, Frank."

"What are we goin' to say?"

"We'll tell him the truth," Hamlin returned without hesitation. "We'll give it to him straight from the shoulder; I don't believe T Bar would risk taking out its vengeance on a fourteen-year-old boy."

"You may be right," Adams nodded.

They settled down to their long ride and put the miles behind them. On arriving at the Wilcox ranch, they found that the two men Adams had sent over were on hand. Wilcox was out in the yard talking with them. He had got a grip on himself and he gave Hamlin and the others a hearty greeting.

"You're here in good time," he told them. "Jest put your horses up to the rack. The boy's in the kitchen helpin' his ma git breakfast for us. Been a long time since we had such a crowd as this here."

They ate hurriedly—fried beef, hot bread, prunes and black coffee. Mrs. Wilcox pressed them to eat more. She was a thin, nervous little woman, old beyond her years with hard work and the loneliness of ranch life. Her son was a clean-looking youngster, reduced to silence by the presence of the company and his involvement in what had transpired the previous morning. He wanted to accompany his father to the Blue Flats.

"Your place is here today with your mother," Hamlin told him. "I wouldn't go too far from the house, Ritchie. You don't have to be afraid; nothing is going to happen to you."

The assembled men got into the saddle and with Wilcox showing the way, they crossed his range to what he called the Blue Flats. They were as level as a billiard table, unscarred by erosion, and bounded on the east and south by the big bend of Squaw Creek. Hills to the northwest, green with cedar and pine, were high enough to offer some protection against the bad storms of winter.

"No wonder Wilcox wants to hold on to this," Roberts observed to Hamlin. "It wouldn't take eighteen acres of grass like this to keep a steer fat and sassy. If this is Government land, why hasn't he bought it?"

"I don't suppose he can swing it. There must be four to five sections of land on these flats. Even at a dollar and a half an acre, that calls for money."

"Tark's got money. I'm surprised he hasn't bought the Blue Flats."

"He wants them for nothing. That's cheaper than buying them, Skip."

Roberts had sparked an idea in Hamlin's mind and he pursued it as they moved up the creek until they found a spot in the scrub timber along the bottoms that offered concealment and also gave them a vantage point from which to watch the flats. He could buy the range and lease it to Wilcox. In a few years he would have his investment back and still own it. He wanted to stop Jeptha Tark. Snatching the Blue Flats out of his greedy hands wouldn't do it. But it would be a step in the right direction. A jab here, and another there, that was the way to do it. They might not hurt too much at first, but they would add up.

They had been waiting a long time, without seeing any sign of T Bar. Out on the flats, Wilcox's cattle grazed contentedly.

"I don't know what to make of it," Adams declared impatiently. "I was sure they'd be here long before this."

"They'll come, Frank," Hamlin asserted unequivocally. "We'll wait all morning if we have to."

It was only a few minutes later that they saw a rider moving toward them from the direction of the house. Wilcox was first to recognize him.

"That's my boy Ritchie!" he cried. "There's somethin' wrong!"

They rode forward to meet him.

"Pa, they're at the house—Tark and a bunch of his men!" the lad got out excitedly. "I was down the crick a bit when I saw 'em comin' from the west. I caught up my horse and lit out as quick as I could—"

They didn't wait to hear any more. Lifting their horses to a sharp hand gallop, they lined out for the Wilcox house, a little more than a mile away. Hamlin surmised that Tark and his riders had gone down Black Tail, stopping to make inquiries at other ranches, before cutting across the basin for Squaw Creek. He was satisfied that it explained why they were late in showing up and why they came in from the west rather than across the Blue Flats. He learned that afternoon that it was exactly what they had done.

"Dallas," Adams shouted to make himself heard above the drumming of their horses' hoofs, "you leave it to Pierce to do the talkin'! Don't go for a gun 'less he says so!" When Wilcox signified his acceptance of the order, Adams got Hamlin's attention. "We'll back you up all the way!"

Mrs. Wilcox had had time to lock herself in. When Hamlin and the others turned the corner of the house, two T Bar riders were hammering on the front door, threatening to break it down unless she opened up. Tark sat on his horse a short distance back, with the rest of his men. Hamlin charged into the pair at the door and sent them flying. Whipping his mount around, he bore down on the master of T Bar. With no more than six feet separating them, they sat there, face to face, their cold, glittering eyes slits of hatred. It was like steel striking steel.

Tark recognized Frank Adams and most of the others. He had not expected to find anyone there but Dallas Wilcox and his family. He counted them, eight in all; he only had four of his crew with him. If it caused him any uneasiness, coming on top of the killing of one of his punchers and last night's incident, he gave no sign of it.

"You have no business with Mrs. Wilcox," Hamlin

said with a wicked coolness. "But threatening and abusing women comes natural to a low-down skunk like you. It reminds me of what my mother suffered at your hands. When I think of it, every drop of blood in me cries out that I'll know no peace until I've made you pay for what you did to her."

"I been called hard names before," Tark returned with counterfeit complacency. "That don't git anywhere with me. Git out of the way and let me talk to Wilcox and Adams."

"Pierce will do the talkin' for me and the rest of us," Wilcox informed him.

"What! This young pup, scarcely dry behind the ears is back a day or two and you men have given him the right to speak for you?"

Jep Tark's tone was scoffingly incredulous.

"You heard right," Adams said flatly. "You got anythin' to say, say it to him."

Jep still couldn't believe it. The ignominy of being reduced to addressing himself to his stepson made him writhe.

"You know why I'm here," he growled.

"I do," Hamlin acknowledged, "and you know why we're here. Your days of doing as you please in Yellowstone Basin are over. It may take a little time for that to get through your head; but it will. You sent Dawson over yesterday to tell Dallas that he had twenty-four hours to get his stuff off the Blue Flats; that you were moving in. They had an argument. Dallas ordered your man to get off the place. He wasn't armed; Dawson was. When Dallas started for the house to get a gun, your man drew on him. This boy was standing in the doorway. When he saw that his father was about to be shot down before his eyes, he snatched up a rifle and killed Len Dawson."

"Good Christ!" Jep jeered raucously. "You don't expect me to believe that tale, do you?"

"You better believe it." Hamlin's tone was deceivingly quiet but there was no mistaking the warning it carried. "If you don't want to find yourself decorating the end of a rope, Mr. Tark, you make it your business to see that no harm comes to Ritchie Wilcox."

The T Bar punchers began to shift about uneasily in their saddles. They were not gunslicks, but they were hard men, and they rode for the brand only because they had proven themselves cut to Tark's pattern. They wondered how much more the old man was going to take from Hamlin. They had seen him explode without warning. But the odds had always been in his favor. Being practical men, they tried to calculate what their chances would be this morning. They didn't find them to their liking.

Tark's face was dark with his thinking. He was doing some calculating too. He had not regarded Pierce Hamlin's return to the basin as something to be taken seriously. He realized now that he had underestimated the man. Young he might be, but there must be something to him to convince hard-headed men like Frank Adams and Tom Lockhart that their interests could be entrusted to him. Lockhart wasn't there, but two of his punchers were, and that was indication enough for Jep. With his eyes boring into Hamlin, he said:

"I reckon I have you to thank for what happened in the T Bar yard last night. What was it supposed to prove?"

"That you're not as high and mighty as you think you are. The idea of a handful of two-bit stockmen invading the sacred precincts of T Bar! We figured that would get under your hide. And it's only the beginning. I'm telling you now: keep your hands off the Blue

Flats. Dallas Wilcox has been using that range for years, and we mean to see that he continues to use it."

"Is that so?" the old man taunted. "Maybe I've got a little surprise up my sleeve for him."

Saying no more, he raised his hand to his men and they thundered out of the yard at a rocking canter.

"You handled him fine!" Adams declared warmly. "Wait till they hear about it this afternoon at the meetin'. It'll show 'em what we can do if we pull together."

Wilcox was pleased too, but he had Tark's parting shot ringing in his ears.

"What do you figger he meant about havin' a surprise up his sleeve for me?"

"Just some more of his big talk to save face," Adams averred. "Pierce was givin' him a bad time."

"I'm not so sure there isn't more to it than that," said Hamlin. "When we were out on the flats, Skip brought up something that may be the answer. He asked me why you hadn't bought that piece of fine range, Dallas—"

"You know why," Wilcox broke in.

"Of course. He asked me then why Tark hadn't grabbed it. It's my long-shot guess that that's what he means to do, now that he sees he's running into some real opposition."

The threat was real enough to silence Wilcox and Adams for a moment.

"Don't let that throw you, Dallas; he hasn't got it yet," Hamlin continued. "If I can get to town ahead of him, I'll buy the Blue Flats and lease the land to you at terms you can afford to pay. When this trouble is over and things are good with you again, I'll sell to you at what I pay. I'm not interested in making a dime out of it."

Wilcox was overwhelmed and didn't quite know what to say. "That's decent of you, Pierce—mighty decent!"

"That's all right, Dallas." Hamlin glanced at his watch. "It's not nine o'clock yet. If I go now, I should be in Broken Rock by noon. That'll give me time enough to get back for the meeting." He glanced at Roberts. "You go with me, Skip. We'll get fresh horses at Cross Keys."

Adams was pleased with him. He had seen enough to convince him that they had found a real leader in Pierce Hamlin. "The rest of us better stick around an hour or so, in case Tark may turn back, figgerin' we'll all be pullin' out."

"Do that, Frank. Skip and I will be on our way."

They were in Broken Rock a few minutes before twelve. After stopping at the bank for a few minutes, they hurried on to the sheriff's office.

"Things have been happening in the basin, Lin," Hamlin said at once. "I'll fill you in a little later. Right now, I want to ask you just one question: has Tark any particular drag at the Land Office?"

"He ain't been doin' any business with the agent, that I know of; but he's certainly acquainted with Dennis McCabe. Why do you ask?"

"When I indicate the sections I want and produce the money to pay for them, I don't want McCabe to do any stalling. Do you mind walking over with us?"

"No, not if you figger it'll give you some moral support. Of course if Tark has been in ahead of you, there'll be nothin' you can do about it."

They caught McCabe the agent, and his collector, closing the office to leave for dinner. McCabe invited them to come back that afternoon.

"You better take care of this man now," Lin Bible urged. "He's come a long way. How long will it take you?"

The agent gave in grudgingly. Hamlin was glad he had the sheriff with him. Once inside, McCabe opened his books and spread his maps on the counter. Hamlin saw at a glance that the sections he wanted were still open. He pointed them out and McCabe then marked them sold. Hamlin walked down the counter to the collector, paid the requested amount and the Blue Flats were his. It was as simple as that, but as he was turning to leave, Jeptha Tark hurried in.

The master of T Bar could not repress a grunt of dismay at finding Hamlin there. The wide grin of sardonic satisfaction on the latter's face told him he had been outsmarted. He didn't know what Lin Bible had to do with it, but the mere presence of the sheriff, an enemy of long standing, further infuriated him.

Bible couldn't forego saying with purring irony, "I guess you're next, Jep."

The old man's jaws clicked together on a wolfish snarl. Rocking with rage, he turned to the door and stormed out.

Later, walking back to his office with Hamlin and Roberts, the sheriff said with immense soberness: "Wherever you ride after this, Pierce, you want to look back over your shoulder once in a while. You stung him, and he won't forget it."

"I'll do my best to make sure he doesn't, Lin. When I've finished with you, Skip and I will grab a quick bite and head for the basin; I want to be back at Tom Lockhart's by three o'clock."

They turned into the office. Hamlin had no hesitancy in acquainting him with the killing of Len Dawson, the T Bar puncher, and its aftermath.

"I know you'll want to talk this over with the prosecutor, Lin. I presume there will be an investigation. Will it be necessary to bring the Wilcox boy in for questioning?"

"That'll depend on what Tark does. If he brings a charge, the boy will have to be brought in. I wouldn't worry about it; as you tell it it was a justifiable killin'." The sheriff leaned back in his chair and gave him a shrewd, puckered glance. "Just what is the connection between what happened at the Wilcox place and your hurryin' into town to buy the Blue Flats?"

"Just about what you're thinking," Hamlin replied, with a flickering half-smile. His account of what had occurred at the Wilcox ranch that morning had Lin Bible nodding approvingly to himself.

"You hit hard and fast, Pierce. I figgered you would. Dumpin' that dead man in the T Bar yard musta given Tark somethin' to think about." The sheriff shook his head over the audacity of it. "Jest don't overstep yourself."

"I'll try not to," Hamlin assured him. He motioned to Roberts and they got up to leave.

"If I want to git in touch with you, where will I find you?" the sheriff asked, as he walked to the door with them.

"Cross Keys for the present."

They found a short-order restaurant that looked clean. As they sat at the counter, Roberts observed that nothing had been said about the meeting scheduled for that afternoon.

"Was that intentional, Pierce?"

"Definitely. Lin's with us all the way, but in his position, he can't take sides openly. I wasn't going to em-

barrass him by telling him anything that he might pre-
fer not to know."

Silence descended on them as they ate out their hunger. Twenty minutes later, they were in the saddle
again and heading for the basin.

6

The number of horses tethered around the corrals, at the far end of the yard, indicated that most of the owners who had been invited to the meeting had already arrived.

Carla was on the gallery with her mother. She stepped out for a word with Hamlin and Roberts as they were about to pass the house.

"How did it go in town, Pierce?"

"Fine," he answered, thinking how cool and pretty she looked this afternoon. "I had the right hunch about that Blue Flats range; Tark was in town to buy it. I had just finished in the Land Office when he barged in. He was fit to be tied. You'd have enjoyed it, Carla."

"I daresay I would. Everyone is here. They came early. You'll find them down under the cottonwoods at the creek. Maybe it's just as well you're a bit late; Frank Adams and Dad have been giving them a talking to." Her smile was encouraging and somehow tender. "I wish you luck, Pierce."

They found the men gathered under the trees, some seated on the bank of the creek, where it was cool, and a little group gathered about Tom Lockhart and Adams. The former introduced Hamlin, where that was necessary. There were only two or three who couldn't remember him as a boy in the basin. He shook hands with Wick Burnett.

"I'm glad you're here," he told him. "I hope we can pull together."

"It won't be my fault if we don't," was Burnett's breezy answer. "With my little ragtag outfit, my opinions don't carry much weight in the basin, but I admire the way you pitched into T Bar. If I can be any help to you, let me know."

Hamlin couldn't decide at once whether he liked the rather slight, blond man or not. If he couldn't be called handsome, he at least had a pleasing face. He smiled easily for one who, according to report, was being hard-pressed to keep his head above water. Hamlin wondered about that as Lockhart walked aside with him.

"They're impressed with the way you've handled yourself so far, Pierce," he said confidentially. "I believe if you give 'em a strong talk, they'll fall into line."

Hamlin acquainted Lockhart with what had happened in Broken Rock.

"That ought to do it!" the latter declared enthusiastically. "It ought to be enough to convince 'em that with you crackin' the whip, we can win this fight and have peace in the basin again. I'll say a few words and tell them the news about Blue Flats before I call on you. We can git started right now."

He got the attention of the crowd.

"I don't want to steal Pierce's thunder," he began, "but you all know what he went to town for. I figger you're entitled to hear how he made out. Jep Tark went in for the same purpose, but it appears that he got there a bit too late; Pierce had the papers signed, sealed and ready to shove down the old Pirate's gullet!"

The crowd cheered, especially Dallas Wilcox.

"Thank God!" Wilcox cried, leaping to his feet, his voice breaking with emotion. "I'll never forget what you done for me, Pierce!"

"Keepin' T Bar off the Blue Flats will mean almost as much to Frank Adams and Homer Knox as it will to you," Lockhart declared. "It's goin' to stop Tark from movin' down Squaw Crick. All three of you have got a lot to be thankful for. But here's Pierce. You listen to what he has to say."

Hamlin knew how to express himself, his earnestness making up for whatever polish he lacked. He realized that his audience understood why he had returned to Yellowstone Basin and what he hoped to accomplish. As for the argument he advanced, it followed closely what he had said the previous day to Lockhart, Adams and Price Pickens.

"If we'll pledge ourselves to support one another," he went on, "we haven't any reason to fear Jeptha Tark. I think the past forty-eight hours proves that. I'm not interested just in stopping him where he is; I want to see him pushed back to where he was before he began grabbing other men's range and hogging the basin."

"That's the ticket!" Pickens called out. "There ain't no point in organizin' unless we got guts enough to run that rat back into his hole, no matter what it costs!"

Three or four echoed that sentiment; others were silent; only Alva Williams, the Black Tail stockman, a man of some importance in the basin, spoke out against it.

"We're talkin' about somethin' now that'll mean bloodshed and killin'," he argued. "Mebbe we can lick Tark and git back what's rightfully ours: the price will be high. I'm ready to pay it, if the rest of you are, but we better give some thought to what we're gettin' into before we go flyin' off the handle. Don't any of you say you'll go into this with the idea that you'll back out later if the goin' gits too tough." He glared about angrily. "It'll be too late for backin' out; we'll be riskin' everythin' we got, and we'll have to see it through, no matter what."

"I agree with every word of that," Hamlin told them, his voice charged with a grim austerity. "I couldn't put it better myself. We'll have a long, hard fight ahead of us. Make no mistake about that."

He spoke of the difficulties they would face and the inevitable setbacks they would encounter, hoping thereby to discover just how far they were prepared to go. With growing satisfaction, he saw that they were not to be easily discouraged; they had had a little taste of victory and it had fired them up as nothing else could have done.

An organization was quickly effected. At Hamlin's request, an advisory committee of three was elected—Lockhart, Adams and Alva Williams—with whom he could be in almost constant touch. An arrangement was also arrived at by which word could be swiftly relayed back and forth across the basin.

The meeting dragged on. Half a dozen suggestions were advanced as to where the first blow should be struck.

"We better not decide on anythin' this afternoon," said Lockhart, when the argument had continued for some time. "Give Pierce and the committee two or three days to talk things over. When we git set on somethin', word will be flashed to you and we'll move so fast T Bar won't have no idea where we're strikin'."

"Tom," Wick Burnett spoke up, "there's been considerable talk about one of us being a spy. You sound as though you thought there was somethin' to it."

"It wasn't my idea, but I'm afraid I got to go along with it," Lockhart replied, the set of his mouth betraying an obscure resentment.

"It was my idea," said Hamlin, his glance fastening on the blond man from Box Elder with a close attention. He was glad the matter had come up. He couldn't say why, but he hadn't expected Burnett to mention it. "If what's been said and done here this afternoon is reported to Jep Tark, it'll really be a favor to us. He won't sleep any better for it. But I wouldn't like for him to know our plans a day or two ahead of time."

"I should say not!" Burnett returned heartily. He was suddenly sober. "It's a damned unpleasant feeling to think you're riding with a man who's out to double-cross you. You must have some idea who he is."

The others had stilled their voices and were listening, looking first one way and then the other, not knowing whom to suspect.

"If I could name him, I wouldn't have waited till now to do it." Hamlin's voice ran cool and even. "He'll be found out soon enough. In the meantime, it leaves the rest of us in the unfortunate position of having to suspect one another. Those of us who are honorable men won't find that too hard to take. If we keep our eyes and ears open, it won't be for long."

The meeting broke up with threats being voiced against the traitor. The men began to leave. Hamlin walked back to the yard with Lockhart and one or two others. Wick Burnett joined them and spoke to Lockhart.

"With your permission, Tom, I'll go up to the house and pay my respects to Carla before I leave."

Lockhart frowned and if he had felt free to do so

would have said no. But ranch hospitality being what it was, all he could do was mutter a grudging: "Go ahead. Tell her we'll be up directly."

Hamlin was not aware of the scowl that darkened his face as he watched Burnett walk his horse up to the house and leave it at the gallery hitch-rack. "And she told me she scarcely knew him," he reflected unhappily. "It doesn't look that way to me!"

With the unfairness of his unconscious jealousy, he wondered what Carla could see in Wick Burnett. He was so engrossed with his thoughts that Price Pickens had to speak to him twice before he got his attention.

"What were you saying, Price?"

"I said it was a mighty big favor you done Dallas, buyin' that range. I'd like to see you do as much for me and Ben Southard."

The others were gone. Hamlin understood now why Pickens had hung on. He smiled at the man's cunning.

"It'll take more than buying a little range here and there to win this fight, Pierce."

"I reckon that's so," the little man agreed. "But it makes as much sense to buy a few thousand acres on Ten Mile as on the Squaw. Stoppin' Tark from coming any further down Squaw Crick means that he'll be puttin' the heat on somewheres else. And it won't be on Box Elder; there ain't enough good range left over there to interest him too much. There's no more easy pickin's on Black Tail. That leaves only Ten Mile. Jest as sure as yo're standin' there, that's where he'll make his next grab."

There wasn't any doubt of it in Hamlin's mind, but he was careful not to say so.

"If T Bar comes at you, Price, you know what to do. Get word to us and we'll be there in a hurry, and strong enough to throw them off."

Pickens had to be satisfied with that. He caught up his horse and left.

"You wasn't givin' him any information," Roberts remarked. "Still a question in your mind about him?"

"What?" Lockhart interjected, showing his surprise. "You suspicious of Price?"

"I was, Tom, but not after last night. I think we'd do well not to divulge any plans to him ahead of time; he talks too much. He's right though about the Ten Mile country. I figure that's where we can expect trouble to come."

"I'm glad you feel as you do about Price," said Lockhart. "He's hard to git along with—some folks don't like him on that account—but he's honest. I thought we were goin' to git by without anythin' bein' said about this spy business. It surprised me to have Burnett bring it up, seein' that nobody knows much about him. I wonder what his idea was."

"I don't know—unless he's the guilty man and thought that would be a good way to throw suspicion away from himself—not that I have any reason to think he is," Hamlin added in fairness. "I must say he looks you in the eye when he speaks to you."

"And gives you his big smile," Roberts muttered sarcastically. "If that ain't a tinhorn smile, I never saw one."

They reached the house a few moments later and found Burnett seated on the gallery with Carla. Whatever it was he was saying, he didn't bother to finish, as Carla ran up to congratulate Hamlin.

"Wick tells me the meeting went your way, Pierce! I'm awfully happy it did!" She was pretty in her excitement and grave too, for she realized the price they might have to pay for taking the offensive against T Bar. "I only hope you can hold the basin men together until the fight's won. They're all for you today; that may not be the case a few weeks from now."

Hamlin's smile was suddenly dangerous. He hadn't expected to hear a discouraging note struck so soon. He flicked an unfriendly glance at the blond man from Box Elder.

"Carla, is that what Mr. Burnett has been telling you?"

"Why—" she began and then hesitated.

"I wasn't stating anything but the facts, Hamlin," Burnett answered for himself. "You know it's true; it's exactly what Alva Williams was throwing up to them— backing out when the going got tough. I know Alva and Frank and Tom, here, and I'll include myself, will stick it out. I ain't so sure about Pickens and two or three others."

"A few may blow hot and cold," Tom Lockhart grunted, as he sat down heavily and motioned for Hamlin and Roberts to be seated, "but they've given their word and there won't be any backslidin'."

The conversation became general and, thanks to Carla, it took on at least a surface friendliness. It grew late, but the visitor hung on. Hamlin wondered if he meant to force an invitation to supper.

"If I'm not being too inquisitive," Hamlin ventured, "how did you happen to land in the basin, Burnett?"

"Oh, I'd been looking for a small place," was the easy, smiling answer. "I didn't have much money. When I saw Drew Oliver's ranch and Box Elder Creek, I fell in love with the place. I like to hunt and fish a bit; it was just what I'd been looking for."

"But Tark was already spreading out, grabbing everything he could get his hands on. You must have known you were buying trouble."

"I was warned," Burnett admitted. "But I figured if

things didn't get worse than they were I could make out." His shoulders lifted in a self-disparaging shrug. "I'm wiser now than I was then," he laughed. "Seeing that I'm more or less a stranger, I suppose I'll be down on your list of probable suspects."

"I'd say that was a fair assumption," Hamlin replied. "You and a good many others."

"You can check my record as much as you please," the blond man invited. "It'll be all right with me. As a matter of fact, Jep Tark has more reason to hate me than he does any of you. But that's neither here nor there as far as you folks are concerned."

He didn't explain his cryptic remark. Mrs. Lockhart came to the door to call them in to supper. She invited Burnett to stay. Hamlin expected him to accept, but, to his surprise, the Box Elder man begged to be excused. He said good evening and they heard him riding away as they reached the table. The crew had come through the kitchen and were already seated.

"I'm sorry Mr. Burnett couldn't stay," said Mrs. Lockhart.

"Mother, he couldn't stay, not after the way he was treated." Carla's voice trembled with indignation. "I don't know what you men have against him. Is it because he likes to hunt and fish and read a book once in a while that you're so down on him? I believe you resent him only because he isn't everlastingly talking about cows and grass. If you know anything to his discredit, what is it?"

She looked first to Hamlin and then to her father. The former was silent; there was nothing on which he could pin the doubts he entertained about Wick Burnett. Lockhart found his tongue.

"You cool down a bit, missy," he admonished. "I don't know anythin' agin him, but I don't like the man.

You'll have to be satisfied with that. I don't know what
he's got to be always smilin' and laughin' about. Lord
knows the rest of us ain't findin' anythin' to be so chip-
per about these days. If anythin' was said out on the
gallery that got under his skin, I'm sorry. We'll let it go
at that; I don't want to hear no more about it."

He knew from experience that Carla could not be
silenced in that manner. She always managed to have
the last word, and she had it now.

"I'm not surprised, Dad, that you and Pierce don't
want to hear any more about it, inasmuch as the worst
you can say against Wick Burnett is that you don't like
him," she said with cutting inflection. "You've certainly
made your point. If you proceed along those lines," she
added sarcastically, "I'm sure you'll have no trouble
finding your spy."

Her father threw up his hands in surrender.

"All right! All right!" he said. "Have it your way,
and let's git on with supper."

Later, with evening coming on, he sat out on the
gallery with Hamlin and Roberts. They were agreed
that nothing was to be gained by waiting for T Bar to
make the first move.

"We better git hold of Frank tomorrow and ride
down to Alva's in the afternoon," Lockhart advised.

"We'll have to work out somethin'."

Wick Burnett's name kept getting back into the conversation.

"Carla is right," said Hamlin. "Disliking the man
isn't enough; we've either got to get hold of something
that'll back up what we're thinking, or forget it."

"The way to do it is to turn spy and watch him for a
couple of days," Roberts drawled. "It's my opinion it'll
pay off."

"It won't hurt to watch him," Hamlin agreed. "We'll

do that, Skip, first chance we get. We can get into the Buckskins and lay out with a pair of glasses. I don't want to be away for a couple of days right now." He turned to Lockhart. "Tom, what did you make of that crack of his about Tark having reason to hate him."

"I didn't pay no attention to it. I thought he was just braggin'."

"I don't know," Hamlin muttered dubiously. "It didn't strike me that way."

7

Buck Ross, the Cross Keys puncher, said at breakfast: "They musta had quite a rain up in the Buckskin Hills last night. The crick's sure runnin' muddy this mornin'."

It occurred so frequently that Lockhart said, "It'll clear up by noon," and didn't give it a second thought.

He went out to have a look at his cattle. Hamlin and Roberts accompanied him. They were gone three hours or more. Coming in from the east, they reached the ranch bridge. Hamlin pulled up when he saw the condition of the creek.

"That don't look right to me, Tom," he said with some anxiety.

"Me neither, Pierce! That's yellow mud it's carryin'. Couldn't have been a cloudburst up in the hills or some dead brush would be comin' down."

"Anyone doin' any irrigatin' up above you?" Roberts asked.

"Oh, Alva's wife and one or two other wimmen irrigate a truck patch. That wouldn't account for it."

"I'm sure it wouldn't," Skip agreed. "Looks to me like someone's tamperin' with the crick."

It rang an alarm in Hamlin's mind. He turned sharply on Lockhart.

"Tom, has Jep Tark ever threatened to throw a dam across Black Tail?"

"No. Black Tail originates on his land, but he's got

no more right to it than we have. Black Tail is a flowin' stream; no man can dam it up without the consent of the other water users. That's the law."

"I know it. But the law wouldn't mean anything to him—"

"Good God!" the other burst out, angrily excited now. "Are you suggestin' that Tark's puttin' up a dam?"

"That could be the explanation. There's no reason to get worked up about it till we know what the facts are. It could be that a piece of bank has caved in. Alva. Williams will likely be able to tell us something this afternoon."

"I suppose so," Lockhart replied soberly, "but you got me worried."

Word had been sent to Adams that he was to join them at Cross Keys, later in the day.

As they neared the house, they saw a horse tethered at the gallery hitch-rack. Lockhart thought he recognized the animal.

"That looks like Lin Bible's roan. I wonder what he's doin' here?"

They found the sheriff seated with Carla and Mrs. Lockhart. He greeted them affably and did not appear to have anything of importance on his mind. But appearances were often deceiving where he was concerned.

"I'm on the way over to talk to the Wilcox boy," he informed them. "Just routine questioning. I had a long talk with the prosecutor, Pierce. No charge has been made and he says he'll let the matter drop if I so advise."

"That's what you'll do, I take it."

The sheriff nodded. "I reckon you can take that for granted. There was another reason why I stopped in."

He glanced at Carla and her mother in such a way that
Mrs. Lockhart said:

"If you have some business to discuss, Carla and I
will step into the house."

"Mebbe you better, Hattie." He told the men to sit
down. When they were alone, he went on, his manner
becoming sober. "Joe Strahorn was in town this
mornin' to meet the eastbound express from Miles
City. He had horses with him. Some fellas got off the
train; he was waitin' for 'em. There was five of 'em. I
recognized two—Cass Nabors and Van Bollinger—the
Miles City gunmen. I figgered if the other three was in
that company they were five of a kind. Strahorn left
town with them a few minutes later, headed for T
Bar." Bible looked about. "I don't know what you
make of it, but I figgered you ought to be told."

No one was in a hurry to speak.

"I ran into Price Pickens on the way out this
mornin',' the sheriff continued. "He told me you fellas
had organized a protective association. These gunmen
look like Jep's answer."

"It couldn't be, Lin," said Hamlin. "That is something he had started before I got back to Montana.
Just figure it out. You must remember that he drove
into Broken Rock that first afternoon. I know he was
home the following night; and yesterday he showed up
at Dallas Wilcox's place. It would take him a couple of
days to go down to Miles City and back and hire those
men. It can't have anything to do with the steps we
took yesterday afternoon."

The sheriff pulled thoughtfully at his mustache for a
moment or two and failed to find any holes in Hamlin's
argument.

"I'm afraid I'll have to agree with you, Pierce.

Tark's evidently got somethin' goin' that you folks know nothin' about."

"I don't know what it could be," Lockhart muttered dismally.

"Mebbe the condition of the crick is the explanation," said Skip Roberts. "Pierce thought it might be."

They informed Lin about the heavy discoloration of Black Tail and he suggested at once that they have another look at it. They found it still running yellow.

"It's not as bad as it was," Hamlin pointed out, "but that yellow muck has been coming down since early morning, and it's noon now."

Lockhart bit back an anguished grunt as he stared at the swiftly flowing water, the lifeblood of Cross Keys. The damming of Black Tail would ruin him, and Alva Williams and half a dozen other men as well. He could no longer doubt that that was what Tark meant to do. "He's buildin' a dam, sure enough, and bringin' hired gunslicks to protect it. What are we goin' to do, Lin?"

"I'd expect you to gather your forces and go up there some night and blow it to hell. If I wasn't wearin' this badge, I'd say that was the thing to do. But you better hold off till you see what the court will do. If he is enjoined, and he ignores it—and he doubtless will—then he won't have a leg to stand on, no matter what happens." He glanced at the sun. "Hattie ought to have dinner on the table in a few minutes. I'm invitin' myself to stay and I'm changin' my plans; I'm goin' up to T Bar first." He glared at Hamlin and Skip. "You fellas raise your right hands; I'm swearin' you in as my deputies for the day; you'll go with me."

As they proceeded up Black Tail, they found Alva Williams and his neighbors in a high state of excitement over the condition of the creek.

"When it didn't begin to clear up by noon," said Williams, "I figgered it could only mean that Tark was runnin' up a dam."

"Keep your shirt on, Alva," Bible advised. "We're on our way to T Bar right now. He won't git away with this if I can stop him."

"Will you be comin' back this way, Lin?"

"No, we'll swing over to the Squaw; I want to question the Wilcox boy. We'll be back at Cross Keys toward evenin'. Mebbe you better be there; I understand Frank Adams will. We'll have a talk."

"If he *is* buildin' a dam, you know where to look for it, don't you?"

"At the mouth of the little canyon where Tark used to have a line camp in the old days. It couldn't be anywheres else."

They went on. The basin pinched up into occasional ridges as it began the upward slanting to carry it into the Buckskin Hills. The undulations of the land were just steep enough to prevent their getting a long-distance view of the country ahead. The bunches of cattle they passed told them they were on T Bar range. On cresting the fourth ridge, the sheriff pulled up and pointed ahead.

"I can see the old cabin from here," he said. "Git out your glasses, Pierce, and see if there's any activity there."

"There sure is!" the latter declared as soon as he had the glasses adjusted. "Wagons are moving up to both walls of the canyon and dumping earth and rock into the creek. Take a look."

"The brass of him!" Bible snorted, as he got the binoculars focused on the mouth of the canyon. "As well as I know the mean old bastard, I couldn't believe he'd have the crust to dam up Black Tail! He's just pouring fill into the canyon, no sign of head-gates. In two or three days, there won't be a drop of water goin' down below. Even a low dam will hold it back for seven, eight weeks, and that'll be the finish of Tom Lockhart and the rest!"

The contours of the country made it evident that by then T Bar would have a lake a quarter of a mile wide and twice as long.

"We'll destroy it, Lin. We'll have to." Hamlin's face was grim.

"Don't tell me what you're goin' to do," Bible snapped. "I don't want to know. We'll go on now till we git stopped. You let me do the talkin', and don't git itchy fingered."

A few minutes later, they rode out of a little swale. Two men rose up from the brush, rifles in hand.

"That'll be far enough," one of them called out. "This is closed range. Just turn around."

The sheriff recognized the speaker.

"Not so fast, Nabors. I'm Lin Bible, the sheriff of this county, and these fellas are my deputies."

The gunman was taken aback to be addressed by name. "Come in a little closer and keep yore hands away from yore guns."

He conferred with his companion as the sheriff and his deputies advanced. He put his hostility aside on seeing the silver star on Bible's vest.

"Yo're Lin Bible, shore enough. Reckon you got the right to go where you want."

"Is Joe Strahorn out here on this job?" Lin asked.

"He's back there bossin' the work."

"Then you take us to him, Nabors. I'll do my talkin' to him."

The T Bar foreman, a scowling six-footer, with a face that looked like it had been chipped out of granite, ran his eyes over the unwelcome visitors with a cold, calculating regard. Lin Bible he knew; he had never seen Hamlin or Roberts before.

"I want you to escort us to the house, Joe," the sheriff informed him. "I got business with Jep."

Without changing expression, Strahorn said: "You been here before, Mr. Sheriff; you know the way to the house; you don't need me to show you."

"Mebbe I've decided to play my cards a little close to my vest," Lin returned coolly, "that is in view of what's goin' on here, plus the fact that I've already been stopped by some of your hired guns. You catch up your horse and we'll git movin'."

Strahorn was in no hurry to comply.

"Who are these gents you got ridin' with you?" he demanded suspiciously.

"A couple of deputies. I'll be glad to make you acquainted. This is Skip Roberts; the tall cuss over there is Pierce Hamlin."

Strahorn's black eyes narrowed to pin points.

"So you're Pierce Hamlin, eh?" The foreman flung the words out with a wicked, slashing malevolence. "I'm sure glad to meet up with you. I reckon you're here to git an eyeful."

"I'm getting one," Hamlin answered with infuriating self-composure. The lash of it burned into Strahorn. His body kinked at the waist and the urge to kill whipped through him.

Roberts read his thoughts. "Don't try it, mister," he drawled, his lips barely moving. "You put a finger on your gun and I'll kill you."

The quiet confidence that rode the Texan's words produced a smile on Strahorn's rocky face that was both wicked and respectful. He had a dozen men within sound of his voice, but he had no thought of calling on them for help; this was personal between Roberts and him, and he assured himself that it would be taken care of to his satisfaction, though not necessarily today. From what he had heard, he had gathered that this man was a fast gun that Hamlin had brought up from Texas. He was now convinced of it. Ignoring Roberts, he said: "Mr. Sheriff, I'll take you to the house, but you ain't foolin' me a minute, deputizin' men who ain't even citizens of Montana."

"Joe, you let me do the worryin' about that," Bible advised. "Let's be movin'."

No one knew better than Joe Strahorn how completely Annette dominated Jeptha Tark. The lustful old man was more than twice her age. It sickened Strahorn to see him doting over her and being led around like a puppy on a string. He hated the woman for coming between Jep and him and in effect giving him two bosses. He did the work, piled up the profits, and for long he had entertained the idea that one day, and deservedly so, T Bar, or part of it, would belong to him. That hope had vanished since the coming of Annette. In his senile infatuation with her, not the ranch, not even his money, was any longer the important thing in Jep Tark's life; she was his one, indispensable possession.

They had no secrets from Strahorn; he watched them too closely. Annette fancied she had one, but she was mistaken. He knew the old man meant nothing to her; that almost under his nose she was carrying on an affair. It was no more than Strahorn would have expected of a woman of her loose morals, and it would have meant little to him, save for the double-barreled hope that Jep would catch her, or—and better still—that she would suddenly walk out on him.

They were recurring thoughts with the T Bar fore-

man, and they popped into his mind as he led the sheriff and his deputies up the yard and entered the house
to find Tark. There was no one in the office or on the
lower floor. Going to the stairs, he called out and got
an answer from above.

Tark came down a few minutes later. Annette was
with him. It was her almost daily custom to ride
through the hills for an hour or two, in the afternoon.
She was dressed for it now, and for all his hatred of
her, Strahorn couldn't deny that she was attractively
voluptuous in her riding habit. She gave him a brief
nod and went out to her horse, standing at the hitch-
rack.

Jep Tark's lined face grew livid as he listened to
what Strahorn had to say. "You sure they're here
about the dam, Joe?"

"Of course! I wanted to divert the crick till we had
the dam finished. They wouldn't have known about it
till the job was done, if we'd gone about it that way."

"It would have cost eight to ten thousand dollars. I
ain't tossin' that kinda money away, Joe, jest to keep
that scum across the basin from knowin' what I'm
doin'. You show Bible and his so-called deputies to the
office, and git back on the job; I can handle 'em."

Though he was still the slave of his own violent
nature, as cruel and vicious as ever, playing lover to a
young wife at sixty-five was sapping his once tireless
energy and virility——something that had not occurred to
him and which he would have vehemently denied if it
had——and making him lean ever more heavily on Strahorn.

The advantage to T Bar of damming Black Tail was
so great that he had gone ahead with it in full realization of the trouble it would bring him. Had he known,
however, that the fourteen small outfits in the basin

were organizing against him—news of which had been brought to him the previous evening—he would have waited, as he had admitted to Strahorn, until he had crushed one wasp's nest before stepping on another. It was too late for such considerations now; the work had begun and he didn't intend to be stopped by the law or gunfire. He thought he knew what he wanted to say to Lin Bible and Hamlin.

He gave them a frosty nod as they stepped in.

"You'd be more welcome, Lin, if it wasn't for the company you're in," he said, his tone hard and offensive.

"I didn't expect to have any red carpet rolled out for me." Bible leaned over the desk and met the owner of T Bar eye to eye. "Jep, you can't git away with that dam. I'll git a restrainin' order against you tomorrow and be back to serve it."

"You'll be wastin' your time," Tark rapped.

"That may be," the sheriff said imperturbably. "If you fail to obey the order, you'll be on your own, Jep. Yellowstone Basin will git a blood bath that'll bring the troops in from Fort Keogh. If that's what you want, you're goin' about it the right way."

Behind his trimmed beard Tark gave him a thin-lipped smile that was humorless. "I don't scare worth a damn, Lin. I don't mean to build a high dam; the water will soon be flowin' over it."

"It'll be fall before they git any water across the basin. What are they goin' to do for their stock?"

"I don't care what they do. They're gangin' up on me, thanks to this fella here." He indicated Hamlin with a jerk of his head. "They want a fight and they'll git it. We'll see who comes out on top."

The ugly old house had its unhappy memories for Pierce Hamlin. The rear door of the office stood open and he could see into what, in his day, was called the "parlor." Some of the furniture was new. He recognized the rocker that had been his mother's favorite chair. The unpainted walls were papered now, a garish pattern of mingled flowers that reflected Annette's taste, or lack of it. And there was a new square piano. Its polished luxury, reminding him of the unfailing miserliness Tark had shown his mother, filled him with a towering resentment, and his hatred of the man blazed up with a wicked flame. He knew he had to leave; that he couldn't trust himself here much longer. Lin Bible was ready to leave, too. He had declared himself, and so had Tark; it left nothing further to be said.

But Tark wasn't finished. He fastened his piercing eyes on Hamlin. "Now that you're here, Pierce, I'm surprised that you ain't got a mouthful of threats for me. I understand you had plenty to say yesterday afternoon at Cross Keys."

"That comes as no surprise to me," Hamlin said tightly. "I expected your spy to report to you without any loss of time. As for threats, I'll leave them to you. You're a stubborn, wilful man, and you can rant all you please about what you will and what you won't do. You don't fool me. Before I'm through, you'll come to me, begging for mercy, and you won't find any." He caught the sheriff's eye. "Come on, Lin, Let's get out of here!"

8

They struck off across T Bar range for Squaw Creek and the Wilcox ranch. Riding easily permitted them to discuss the dam and the meeting with Tark.

"I'm warnin' you, Pierce, not to make a move till I've had a chance to see what I can do," said the sheriff. "I don't believe Tark is bluffin'. But he may be. It won't take me more'n a day or two to find out. You hold off till then, understand?"

"That'll be all right with us," Hamlin nodded. "If the law can keep the creek open, fine. But it's going to be kept open, Lin. It's a matter of life and death for every outfit on Black Tail."

"You don't have to tell me; I know," Bible growled. "When you told Jep that you wasn't surprised that he knew all about the meetin' yesterday afternoon, was that the truth?"

"It was. We know we got a spy among us. We don't know who he is, but you can see for yourself that we got one."

"That's bad—awful bad!" The sheriff wagged his head solemnly. "It's like havin' a knife at your back and never knowin' when it's goin' to cut you down. You got to weed him out."

"You're acquainted with every man in the basin, Lin. Would you have a hunch—in confidence, I mean?"

A heavy silence descended on Lin Bible as he rode

on, his eyes screwed up in an inscrutable squint. Hamlin was about to repeat his question, when the other finally answered.

"Naw," he muttered, putting temptation aside. "It wouldn't be right to say anything; I don't know enough. This is one of those times when a hunch is no good; you got to have some evidence."

"You're right," Hamlin acknowledged, appreciating the man's fairness.

When they reached the Wilcox ranch, the sheriff went into the house with the boy, after telling Dallas to remain outside. Hamlin took advantage of the opportunity to acquaint Wilcox with the situation on Black Tail. Dallas was all fight this afternoon.

"We got to do somethin', Pierce. Those outfits over there have got to have water. We're too far into summer to git any amount of rain. The water table if near the surface all over the basin, but there ain't time for a man to put down wells, even if he could afford to."

"Something will be done, Dallas," Hamlin assured him. "I can't tell you what just now, but I'll keep you informed."

They were still discussing the matter, and the bringing in of hired gunmen, when the sheriff rejoined them.

"The boy tells a straightforward story, Dallas," he told Wilcox. "You can rest easy; you'll hear no more about it."

Wilcox urged them to stay for refreshments, but the sheriff begged off; the hour was late and they still had a long ride ahead of them. Though they moved right along, the afternoon was gone when they reached Cross Keys. Frank Adams was there, and not only Alva Williams but all the Black Tail owners. When they had heard what Hamlin and the sheriff had to tell them, they were for immediate, violent action.

"I appreciate what you propose to do for us, Lin," said Lockhart, grimly determined, "but I don't believe a dozen court orders would have any effect on Tark. We'll have to take care of this ourselves."

Three or four others expressed themselves likewise.

It was no less than Hamlin had expected. He didn't believe any more than they did that the sheriff's efforts would be successful, but even though they failed, it would give the Association the advantage of having T Bar in open defiance of the law and justify them in taking it into their own hands. The basin men were desperate, in the face of this unforeseen calamity, but he proved his leadership by whipping them into line. Bible went on to town, and the others continued the discussion.

"T Bar is undoubtedly doing what we are—concentrating all attention on the dam," Hamlin declared. "Tark will have his gunmen and as many of his crew as Strahorn can spare waiting there for us. That ought to be as good an opportunity as we could ask for hitting him somewhere else. If you can see it my way, we'll leave tomorrow morning with every man we can muster and head for Ten Mile. We'll go up both sides of the creek and drive T Bar back where it belongs. As soon as Southard and Pickens are in possession of their old range, I'll buy enough of it to block Tark the same way we blocked him on the Blue Flats. Kick that idea around and let me know how you feel about it."

Frank Adams endorsed it at once. Lockhart and the rest of the Black Tail Creek men were so engrossed with their own problems that they were reluctant to put them aside even temporarily, but to strike a telling blow at T Bar in some other direction appealed to them in their bitterness. It took very little persuasion to gain their unanimous support.

"All right," Hamlin summed up. "We'll see how our system for getting word back and forth across the basin will work. Each one of you has a man or two to notify. You know what you're expected to do. Send the word out this evening. All of you be here in the morning, no later than seven o'clock. Bring as many of your men with you as you can—and come armed." He turned to Adams. "Frank, as I remember it, you are the one to notify Burnett. Am I right?"

"Yes—"

"Well, don't fail to do it. I want him here. And now before we break up, I want to warn you not to say anything about our plans for tomorrow—not to anyone. Just tell them they're to be at Cross Keys in the morning; that I'll tell them what we're going to do when they get here. If you want to talk about what's happening on Black Tail, go ahead; that'll be all right. If you'll follow those instructions to the letter, what results will come pretty close to proving whether one of you is Tark's agent, or one of the six who aren't here."

"How do you figger that?" Alva Williams and several others asked.

"That's simple enough," said Hamlin. "If we find T Bar in force on Ten Mile tomorrow it can only mean that they were tipped off; that one of you passed the word to Tark. If we find only a couple of T Bar men in our way, which is what we might reasonably expect, then I'd say we can look for our spy among the half-dozen owners who are not here now. Do you follow me?"

It was not only understandable but obviously so true that they didn't have the temerity to question it.

"That's smart thinkin'," Frank Adams chuckled. "No matter what we run into on Ten Mile, we'll be able to separate the sheep from the goats. In the meantime, it should make the eight of us damned careful not to pass out any information."

Walking up to the house with Hamlin and Skip, after the others had left, Lockhart voiced a question that was irritating him. "Pierce, will you tell me why you made such a point of gittin' word to Burnett?"

"I had a couple of reasons. I want him with us tomorrow so I can watch him. Not to ask him would tell him which way the wind was blowing. If he's guilty, he'll be easier to trap if he doesn't get scary."

Forty strong, owners and hired hands, they left Cross Keys in the early morning and cut across the basin to the valley of Ten Mile Creek. In the past, Southard, to the east of the stream, and Price Pickens, to the west, had used unchallenged as their "customary range" everything in the valley as far up as the Forks. Tark's steady encroachment had pushed them back fully three miles. It was Hamlin's intention, circumstances permitting, to drive all the way up the creek to the Forks, sweeping T Bar completely out of the lower valley of Ten Mile.

On reaching it, he divided his forces and sent half of his men up to the east of the creek, under the leadership of Tom Lockhart. Crossing the stream with the rest, he started moving across Price Pickens' range. He had Pickens with him, and Roberts and Wick Burnett. The latter, now that he knew what was afoot, appeared eager to press on. If he sensed that he was being closely watched, there was nothing in his manner to indicate it.

"I see they're spreading out across the creek," Hamlin called out. "We better do the same; Pike says we'll be seeing T Bar stuff just beyond that line of dead willows."

Breaking through the fringe of dead trees, they saw

little bunches of T Bar cattle grazing a short distance away. It was wild range stock, and when the steers saw the line of advancing riders, they put up their tails and ran. One bunch tried to break through, but they were easily turned.

The drive continued, slow and methodical. In the course of a mile it netted upwards of four hundred head. Lockhart and his men were doing equally as well.

Two Tark riders appeared at a distance. They spurred forward several hundred yards and then pulled up sharply. Seeing what was taking place, and evidently agreeing that two men against a score could do nothing, they wheeled their broncs and disappeared up the creek at a driving gallop.

Burnett dashed up to Hamlin.

"They're going for help, Pierce. We better not get caught out here in the open."

"What would you advise?" was the other's artful query.

"I'd drop back down the creek a bit and find a spot that'll give us some cover."

Hamlin was in doubt as to what prompted the suggestion. It could have sprung from an honest fear for their safety. On the other hand, there was as much reason to believe it was a bid to gain time for T Bar.

"We're not dropping back," he said flatly; "we're going on to the Forks. If we get into a fight, and you don't like the way it's going, you can pull out any time."

"I don't know as there was any call for that," Burnett whipped back. It was the first time Hamlin had seen him angry. "Don't let your head get too big for your hat! While I'm about it, I don't mind telling you that I question what your real purpose is in buying a piece of range here and another there, just to help men out who haven't the money to buy it themselves. Keep it up, and you'll come out of this trouble the boss of Yellowstone Basin. It'll be your heel, not Tark's that'll be on our necks."

Hamlin rode on without attempting to answer. Burnett had brought up something that had not occurred to him. He was quick to see, however, that some men might regard what he was doing in that light. "I'll scotch that idea!" he growled to himself.

They reached the Forks without seeing another Tark rider and joined forces. The basin men were elated. Though not a shot had been fired, there wasn't a T Bar steer left between the Ten Mile Forks and the Yellowstone.

"By grab, we shore took 'em by surprise this time!" Pickens gloated. "The trick now is goin' to be to keep that T Bar stuff from driftin' back!"

"You mean to keep Tark from drivin' it back," Ben Stoddard declared pessimistically. "We're in possession of this range for the minute, Price, but we're a long ways from havin' it nailed down."

"I agree with you, Ben," said Hamlin. "Tark will make an effort to reclaim it. But I'm leaving for town right now, as I told you I would. There isn't more than five or six sections of land in here. If it's open, I'll buy all of it and lease it to the two of you on terms that'll be satisfactory. And with the same understanding I have with Dallas about buying it from me later on for what I pay for it."

"I don't have to tell you, Ben and me appreciate it," Pickens told him. "You may have to wait some time before you git yore money out of this deal."

"That part of it is all right with me, Price. I think I should tell you that it's been thrown up to me that I may

not be buying a piece of range here and there just to help
you men out and stop Jep Tark, but that my real purpose is to build up a big outfit for myself. Nothing
could be further from the truth. The best way to prove
it is for me to put it in writing that I'll sell to you at
cost whenever you're in a position to take it off my
hands."

Burnett was one of the group that surrounded him.
He was silent, but the others without exception reacted
to the scurrilous imputation with vociferous indignation.

"Who in hell threw that up to you?" Lockhart demanded angrily.

Hamlin shook his head. "It doesn't matter, Tom. I
left myself open to it. I'm glad it came up so I could
answer it. I don't think it's necessary to say any more.
I wish you'd take command there till Skip and I get
back from Broken Rock. That won't be before the
middle of the afternoon. If you find you have to use
your guns, don't hesitate. If we can't lick Tark here,
we'll never do it over on Black Tail."

"You'll try to see Bible when you're in town?"
Adams asked.

"If he's there, I'll see him, Frank. I'd like to bring
back some news of how he's making out. I'll get a
drink, Skip," he said to Roberts, "and we can be on
our way."

He walked over to the creek. Adams, Alva Williams
and Lockhart went with him. Having moved all the
way up to the Forks unopposed had them convinced
that the traitor in their camp had not been among
those present at Cross Keys the previous afternoon.

"Of course," Williams pointed out, "Tark could
have been informed and decided the move up Ten Mile

was only a bluff to draw his strength away from the dam and refused to fall for it."

"No, Alva," said Hamlin, "Tark knows we'll never try to destroy that dam by daylight. Our spy is one of the six who wasn't on hand yesterday. I think I could name him right now. But I won't; I want to be sure before I say anything."

At the U. S. Land Office in Broken Rock, Hamlin found the greater part of the valley of Ten Mile Creek open. He bought four and a quarter sections, about equally divided to the east and west of the creek itself.

The sheriff's office was deserted. A little questioning next door elicited the information that Lin had left town hurriedly about ten o'clock.

"That's a good sign," Hamlin told Roberts. "He's evidently got his restraining order and gone to T Bar. I want to drop in at the *Monitor* office and put an ad in the paper, stating I've bought the Ten Mile range. It'll notify Tark that it's no longer in the public domain. We can eat then and start back."

When they returned to the Forks, they found the basin men at ease.

"You had any trouble, Tom?" Hamlin asked at once.

"Wal, Strahorn showed up with most of his crew soon after you left. He ordered us off. I told him we'd have to be driven off; that if he wanted to try it to go ahead. They left after a bit. We ain't seen nothin' of them since. They'll be back tonight, no doubt."

"I'd expect them to," Hamlin agreed. "Some of us will have to stick it out. A dozen will be enough; we don't need forty men."

After he had given them the news from town, he called for volunteers to spend the night on the creek

with Roberts and himself. More than enough responded. Burnett was not among them. Hamlin was just as
well satisfied that he wasn't.

"Ben's here with two men and Price with one; that's
five," said Hamlin. "Counting Skip and myself makes
seven. I'll pick out five more, just to be sure we'll be
strong enough. If we drop back to your place now,
Ben, can your wife give us supper?"

"Of course!" was Southard's hearty response.

"Then we'll go now. It'll give me an opportunity to
put my deal with you and Price in writing. The rest of
you stay here till we get back. You can go to the house
and eat then."

The arrangement was carried out. Lockhart and the
men who were not staying struck off for home. Several
hours of daylight remained. Hamlin saw no purpose in
patrolling the imaginary line that had been agreed on
until night fell.

The sun went down and the long twilight came on.
As it began to fade, Hamlin said: "I guess we better be
moving out. Price, you and Ben take your men and get
across the creek; the rest of us will guard this side. The
moon will be up early. We'll have light enough to see
what we're doing. Two quick shots will be the signal
that T Bar is moving in. If they are fired, it will be up
to all hands to get to the spot as fast as they can."

"I figger we can do better than that by holin' up
somewheres," Pickens demurred. "They'll most likely
stay close to the crick and come down on yore side to
take advantage of the shadders of the trees in the bottoms."

"No," Hamlin objected emphatically. "Do that and
we'll leave the way open for them to get around us.
We'll patrol the line and watch the creek too."

They spread out and moved back and forth, vigilant

and apprehensive. But as the night wore on, it seemed that there was little reason for their anxiety; in the wide sweep of country to the east and west of the Forks nothing moved but themselves. The hour grew late and it lacked only a few minutes of midnight when two quick shots from the gun of Buck Ross, the Cross Keys puncher, shattered the serenity of the night.

Hamlin got to him quickly, closely followed by Skip and the others.

"They're comin' down the crick, close into the trees, like Price said," said Buck. "Listen and you'll hear 'em."

Hamlin cocked an ear. "You're right, Buck. We'll hunt the shadows too."

Pickens and his party came splashing across the creek.

"By grab, I told you!" the little man grunted triumphantly on seeing his prediction borne out.

"You called the turn," Hamlin admitted. "Hold your fire till I give the word."

The oncoming riders stopped and the night grew still again. After what could have been time for consultation, they came on. Presently they reached a break in the trees and in the moonlight, the basin men saw the T Bar crew moving towards them in single file. Hamlin gave the word and a dozen guns crashed. A T Bar horse screamed and went down. Its rider went down with it and after flopping about on the ground lay still. Spattering fire came from the others.

Riding single file offered some protection to the Tark crew, but it placed them at a disadvantage for replying to the attack. They scurried out of the patch of moonlight. Before they could make a charge, another blast from the basin men ripped into them. Apparently convinced that they would have to find a better way of routing the enemy, they suddenly swung their horses and beat a retreat, picking up their dead companion as they fled.

Hamlin looked about at his followers. "Any damage here?"

No one had been struck.

"We sent them packin'!" Price Pickens chortled. "They won't try that again!"

"No, but they'll try something else; they're not giving up that easy," Hamlin observed soberly. "It's my guess that they'll swing over toward the Ten Mile Bluffs and come charging into us full tilt from that direction. We'll have to leave the creek and move out to meet them. It'll be the real thing this time. Open up as soon as you see them, and make it count."

They were a mile west of the creek when Skip Roberts cried: "Here they come!"

With a wild, Texas yell, he charged forward, Hamlin and the others with him, their guns blazing. T Bar came on too, laying down a steady fire. The wicked crashing of gunfire echoed against the bluffs and was flung back magnified tenfold and rolled down the valley of Ten Mile like angry thunder.

Chet Ingalls, one of Ben Southard's punchers pitched out of his saddle, mortally wounded. Sam Rooks, a Black Tail man was struck, not seriously enough to put him out of the fight.

T Bar's headlong rush ground to a stop. Hamlin could see no empty saddles, but at least three Tark riders had swung back out of range. He could only assume that it was because they were no longer able to work a gun. The moonlight was bright enough to enable him to identify Joe Strahorn, keeping his gun bucking as he exhorted the crew to a greater effort. But they had only their dubious loyalty to the brand and their wages to inspire them, and they had had enough. They fired a parting blast that shot Hamlin's horse out from under him and beat a retreat. Pickens wanted to follow them up. Hamlin called him back. The first armed battle with T Bar was over, and it had gone against Tark. He was satisfied to let it go at that.

"You and Ben move your stuff on this grass tomorrow, Pike. I don't believe you'll have any more trouble; Tark will realize when he reads the *Monitor* that he's lost Ten Mile."

They carried Chet Ingalls to Southard's house. He died a few minutes later. It sobered them. But they were steadied by the realization that any one of them could have had a similar fate. Rooks' wound proved to be of no consequence. They cleansed and bandaged it.

Hamlin thanked them for the fight they had made.

"Tark will try to make light of it and call it just the first skirmish, no doubt. He may fool himself into believing it, but I doubt it; we hurt him tonight and he'll remember it. It's after three now. We better be pulling out for home."

Dawn was in the sky when Roberts and he reached Cross Keys. They stopped at the bridge and had a look at Black Tail. It was still running yellow, the amount of water it was bringing down no more than half its usual flow, evidence enough that work on the dam had continued throughout the previous day.

Roberts scowled. "At that rate, she'll be dry in another forty-eight hours."

That was too apparent to be denied. Hamlin nodded grimly. "It's up to Lin Bible; if he doesn't have any luck with Tark, Black Tail will be dry before we can do anything."

9

It was noon when Skip Roberts walked into the bunk-house and shook Hamlin awake. He had been up for several hours and given Lockhart a full account of the fight at the Forks.

"Pull on your clothes, Pierce, and we'll go up to the house; it's almost dinner-time."

"As late as that, eh?" Hamlin had to glance at his watch before he could believe it. "You've talked things over with Tom, I suppose."

"Yeh—"

"How did he take it?"

"Oh, pleased. But he's so damn worried about what he's goin' to do for water that it's purty hard for him to think about anythin' else."

"I can appreciate that," Hamlin remarked, getting into his clothes. "We may get some word from Lin to-day. More likely it won't be before tomorrow. We'll just have to sweat it out."

For his wife's sake and Carla's, Lockhart tried to put as brave a face on the situation as he could when they got to the table. They did likewise. But no one was deceived; all knew that without water Cross Keys could not survive.

"Things are not as bad as they might be," Hamlin said encouragingly. "We've got Tark stopped on both flanks; the next push he makes will have to be down the middle of the basin, and that's where we're strongest."

Carla found little merit in his argument. "Jep Tark will hardly be pushing further down Black Tail if there isn't any water in it, Pierce."

"There'll be water in Black Tail again—as much as there ever was, Carla—and it won't be a matter of waiting eight to ten weeks for it as Tark figures. His scheming isn't hard to see through. When I was in the Land Office yesterday I studied the official map of the basin. He owns the land the dam is on and most of what lies above it. But he's running stock on miles of range below the dam. Though he won't have any water on it for some time, he doesn't mean to give it up. What he's planning on is rotating his cattle; he'll bring a fresh herd in every five or six days. They can make out for that long, and by that trick he hopes to keep occupancy of the range. When his lake fills up, the overflow will start pouring down the basin again."

"Before that happens some of us will have gone bust," Lockhart said heavily.

"I think he's counting on that, Tom, and figuring he can pick up the pieces for little or nothing." Hamlin shook his head incredulously. "It's hard to believe that Tark could let his greed make such a fool of him as not to realize that men like you and Frank Adams and a dozen others would rise up, ready to risk everything, even life itself, sooner than be ground down like that."

"I reckon it's occurred to him by now that he's got a bear by the tail," drawled Skip. "If he's in any doubt about it a couple of dozen sticks of dynamite will convince him."

The shortage of water on Cross Keys had never been desperate enough in the past to cause Tom Lockhart to do anything about catching the run-off from the nest of springs that bubbled out of the ground, a mile and more to the southwest of the house. As he finished dinner, however, he told the crew he would go out with them that afternoon and throw up an embankment.

"If worst comes to worst, some of the stock will have a little water."

"I'll go out with you and give you a hand," Roberts volunteered. "I know Pierce wants to stick close to the house in case word comes from Bible. By the way, Tom, how far are we from the Yellowstone?"

"Oh, it's three miles to the railroad and another three or better to the river." He shook his head, surmising what Roberts had in mind. "You can't water stock along there; too much quicksand. We'll do what we can at the springs, and that's all we can do."

Hamlin was on the gallery when they filed out of the yard, armed with shovels. Carla came out and sat down with him after they had gone. She made a valiant effort to dissemble her anxiety. He admired her courage, but he could see the strain she was under.

"I'm glad you are taking it easy for a change," she said. "You've been on the go ever since you came. We really haven't had a chance to get acquainted."

"It hasn't been a case of out of sight out of mind," he told her, with a bantering smile. "I don't believe I'd like for you to know how often you've been in my thoughts. It might spoil you."

She dismissed it with a laugh, but it brought the color to her cheeks. "I've heard of Irish blarney. Your Texas variety seems to have been chipped off the same stone."

"I don't know about that," he laughed. "Texas was good to me. I'll never forget it."

"You'll go back eventually, of course—"

"I don't know that I will." His tone was suddenly sober. "I haven't looked that far ahead. But this is my home country. When I've brought Jep Tark to his knees, I think I'd like to remain here."

She looked away that he might not see how pleased she was to hear him say it. "I understand Texas girls are very beautiful—"

"They are, but I never met one who was lovelier than you, Carla." Seeing that he had embarrassed her, he added quickly, "I don't suppose I should have said that, even though it's the truth."

He gazed at her fondly as she sat there, eyes lowered, and told himself that she was indeed a rich prize for the man who could claim her.

"I don't know what you think of me—so saturated with hatred and bitterness," he went on. "I've seen something in your eyes at times that told me you pitied me. Perhaps I am to be pitied. I know it's no way for a man to live, but I've lived with it for five years. But now that you see what Tark is doing to you and your folks, perhaps you can appreciate why I feel as I do."

"I do, Pierce—I do!" she murmured earnestly. "I hope some terrible punishment comes to that man. I try not to let dad and mother see, but I'm so scared. I don't know what we'd do if we lost Cross Keys. You're our only hope, Pierce. If it wasn't for you, I don't know what we'd do."

He placed his hand on hers as he saw tears standing in her eyes.

"Carla, no matter what happens, don't lose faith in me," he said deep in his throat. "I take it for granted that I'm a marked man with a price on my head. Sooner or later one of Tark's gunslicks will try to cut me down. Skip understands that as well as I do, and we're prepared for it—"

"Pierce, how can you say that?" she interjected incredulously. "You know there is no such thing as being prepared for a man lying in wait to kill you."

"Knowing he is waiting somewhere comes under the heading of being prepared," he answered quietly. "There is a good rule to follow in such circumstances and I mean to observe it. It's simply this: kill before you get killed. I mean to win this fight, Carla—for your sake as well as my own."

Mrs. Lockhart joined them and the conversation took a lighter turn. She had brought her sewing out with her. Hamlin watched her covertly and decided that Carla wasn't the only member of the family who was making a determined effort to conceal her inner anxiety.

It got to be the middle of the afternoon. There was no sign of Lin Bible. Masking his impatience, Hamlin excused himself and sauntered down to the bridge. Black Tail Creek had been shrinking steadily since early morning. Its channel was now so narrow that there were places where he was sure he could leap across. It emphasized the futility of waiting to hear how the sheriff had made out.

The little bridge had no guard rails. Seated on the edge of the planks, his long legs dangling over the purling stream, he mulled over the several plans that had occurred to him for the counter stroke that he was certain was inevitable now. He settled on one that was no less dangerous than the others but holding the double promise of succeeding and unmasking Wick Burnett as the traitor as well.

The afternoon wore on. Lockhart and the others returned from the springs. He couldn't repress a grunt of dismay as he glanced at the creek. "Lin show up?" he demanded anxiously.

"I haven't seen anything of him, Tom. The answer is right here; it ain't necessary for him to bring it."

Lockhart nodded glumly. "There don't seem to be any question about that. Did you hear anythin' from Price or Ben?"

"No, and that's all to the good; they can't be having any trouble on Ten Mile or they would have got word to us. I've been doing some thinking while I been sitting here, Tom. You and Skip better sit down with me and we'll talk it over."

The Cross Keys punchers took the horses and went on to the corral. Accompanied by Lockhart and Roberts, Hamlin moved over to the shade of the cottonwoods.

"Before I begin," said he, "tell me, is there any quantity of dynamite on the ranch?"

"I got a few sticks, that's all," Lockhart replied. Dynamite was a sobering word. "We can git all we need in town."

"It would be a mistake to buy any right now," Hamlin demurred. "It would be traced back to us. There must be plenty in the basin; everyone must have a little. A couple of dozen sticks and thirty feet of fuse will be enough."

"We can collect that much, I'm sure," said Lockhart.

"We'll do it tomorrow morning. Skip knows how to handle the stuff. We'll need one more experienced man."

"I wouldn't call myself an experienced man, but I ain't afraid of dynamite," Lockhart offered. "I'll—"

"No, Tom, I'd rather not have one of the owners. You'll understand when I explain what I got in mind. How about Buck?"

"Buck Ross has handled some of the blastin' on the

ranch. He'd do a job. You've seen enough of him to know he's got a cool head on his shoulders."

"Buck's a good man," Hamlin agreed.

He began to outline what he proposed doing. The first step was to be a call for all available men to meet early of an evening at Wick Burnett's Box Elder ranch, and from there get into the mountains and work around the basin into the Buckskin Hills. They would move down Black Tail then, by-passing the T Bar house, and attack the dam from that direction rather than moving up the creek for a frontal attack as Tark would have every reason to expect them to do.

"I'll see Burnett personally, tell him what the plan is and swear him to secrecy."

Skip Roberts' mouth curled sarcastically. "That'll be fine! God God, Pierce, you won't no more than have your back turned on him before he'll be makin' tracks for T Bar!"

"That's what I'm counting on him to do," was Hamlin's unruffled comment. "There's a couple of things he won't know, or anyone but us until we leave this place and by then he won't be able to do anything about it. My story to him will be that we're going to follow Box Elder into the mountains and get through the Buckskin Hills so we can come down Black Tail in back of the dam and make an all-out fight of it. I'll tell him nothing about what you and Buck are going to be doing. Knowing we'll be coming down the Creek, Tark will pull his men away from the dam and post them where they can stop us from getting through. We'll bump into them long before we get near the T Bar house. When we do, that'll be as far as we'll try to go; we'll just take cover and keep them busy for forty to fifty minutes. When they see they've got us stopped, they'll be satisfied to shoot it out on those terms."

Roberts began to grin. "I'm beginnin' to git your game now. Buck and me will be a mile or so away, but we'll hear the shootin'. It'll be the signal for the two of us to move up to the dam and start plantin' our dynamite."

"That's the idea, Skip. You'll have to work fast, but as long as you hear the cannonading going on, the two of you will be safe; mine that dam as deep as you can, light your fuses and clear out. The risky part of your job will come when you move up to go to work. Most likely you'll find at least one man left there. You'll have to pick him off. There'll be so much shooting up above that a shot or two at the dam won't be noticed."

"When the charges go off, they'll hear 'em," Lockhart said, thinking aloud. Hamlin's proposed action strongly appealed to him. He could find no holes in it, but he wanted to be sure. "What do you figger will happen then?"

"One of two things. They'll know the dam is gone. That'll stun them some. They may decide to get down there at once to see what the damage is, or they may take the offensive and tear into us. We'll be strong enough to hold them off as we drop back. I don't believe they'll follow us very far."

"Wal, I'm for it, Pierce!" Lockhart declared without further hesitation. "We got to do somethin' and I don't believe we could figger out anythin' better. There's no doubt in my mind that Burnett will walk into the trap. But before we do anythin' we'll have to put it up to Frank and Alva."

"Of course. We can do that tomorrow."

"How much longer you goin' to give Lin Bible?" asked Roberts.

"I'll give him till noon. If we haven't heard from him by then we'll go ahead with our plans. We'll get

Alva down here and go over to the Squaw to Frank's place. If we come to an agreement, I'll go on to Box Elder to see Burnett."

In the morning Black Tail was no more than a trickle. Water stood in the deep holes, but for any practical purpose the creek had stopped flowing. It made waiting for the sheriff to put in an appearance an infuriating experience for the owner of Cross Keys.

It was after eleven before Lin rode in. His dejected manner told them that he had failed.

"I've just come from T Bar," he said. "I was there yesterday too. Pringle (the judge of the District Court in Broken Rock) issued a temporary injunction against Tark, restrainin' him from proceedin' with his dam. When I served it, Jep tore up the paper and flung it on the floor. He told me to tell Pringle to go to hell; that no injunction was stoppin' him. The judge hit the ceilin' and cited him for contempt. That's what took me back to T Bar this mornin'."

"Where does that leave matters?" Hamlin inquired.

"Tark will have to show up in court at ten o'clock tomorrow or I'll have to take him into custody." Bible mopped his brow. The morning was warm. "He'll be there, I figger——with his lawyer. Pringle will fine him, for sure, and he may order him held in the county jail for thirty days."

"Nothing will come of that," Hamlin predicted. "Tark will get a stay and carry the matter to a higher court."

"That's what he'll do," Lin growled. "It'll drag out for months. He'll never go to jail. In the meantime, you folks can go broke. But that's the law for you!"

Lockhart started to speak, but the sheriff stopped him. "Oh, I know you're not goin' to take this lyin' down, Tom, but I don't want you to tell me what your plans are. You know where my sympathies lie. I got to let it go at that; I can't even advise you what to do. The best I can do is wish you luck."

He didn't stay long. A Cross Keys rider was sent to fetch Alva Williams to the ranch. When Alva got there, the four of them, Hamlin, Roberts, Lockhart and he left at once for Squaw Creek to confer with Adams.

The Association's three-man committee unanimously approved Hamlin's plan. Alva Williams was outspokenly in favor of it. "We couldn't settle on a better scheme to blow that dam to hell!" he declared. "You won't have to go lookin' for dynamite; I got plenty. There's no point in waitin' a couple of days; we can be ready by tomorrow night."

"Tomorrow night would be my idea," said Hamlin. "Skip and I will go on over to Box Elder right now. Alva, when you get home, check on the amount of dynamite and fuse you've got on hand. Skip and Buck will be down in the morning to pick it up. If you find you haven't enough it'll give us time to pick up some more from someone else."

He arranged with Roberts that when they were within a mile of Burnett's place he would go in alone. "If you show up with me now, he may get to wondering why you aren't with me tomorrow evening."

"This will be a good place to wait," the Texan drawled, a few minutes later. "I'll move back into that clump of cedars. You watch yourself. You know there's no closed season on you, Pierce."

Hamlin found Burnett at home. The latter was plainly surprised to see him and was guardedly cool, not knowing what to expect after their run-in at the Forks on Ten Mile. His manner changed when the other, with pretended goodwill, informed him of what was afoot and that the Association men would be gathering there the following evening.

When Burnett began to press him for the most minute details, Hamlin understood why. He was happy to supply them.

"What time will you fellows be showing up, Pierce?"

"I imagine some will be here as early as seven. I'd like to pull away about dark. I know you must get into the Buckskins frequently. Will we have any difficulty swinging around to the head of Black Tail?"

"Not a bit. We can make it in about two hours."

Hamlin nodded. "That'll be fine; we'll plan to be moving down the creek by ten o'clock. You understand, Wick, that nothing must get out about this."

"Naturally! You needn't worry about my saying anything, Pierce. I won't have a chance to," he laughed. "Nobody ever comes here. I'd like to show you the ranch. To me, it's the prettiest place in the basin. I can do that some other time; I know you've got a long ride back to Cross Keys."

"Yeh, and I better get started," Hamlin said, taking the hint.

He swung up and rode away without glancing back, but though he was convinced that he had little reason to fear Burnett, he felt easier when he was out of gun range.

Skip was waiting for him. He gave Hamlin a sharp, appraising glance. "I see you look pleased with yourself," he drawled.

Hamlin gave him a crinkly smile. "We're all set with Burnett. He'll do as I expected him to do. There's just one thing I don't understand. What's his pay-off, Skip?"

"Money. What else?"

"I wonder," Hamlin muttered skeptically. "I can't explain it, but I've got the feeling that it's something more than money."

10

At her father's urging Carla and her mother drove into Broken Rock in the morning to do some shopping. They had no heart for it. Without being acquainted with the details, they knew, as every woman in the basin did, that an all-out battle to destroy the dam was to be made that evening, and they were filled with dread when they considered the probable cost. They could only hope and pray with the others that their menfolks would not be among the maimed and killed.

"I thought mebbe it would git their minds off their worries for a few hours," Lockhart explained to Hamlin when they had seen them off. The latter nodded understandingly.

"I hope so, Tom. Waiting is harder on them than it is on us."

During the morning Skip and Buck Ross went down to Alva's for the dynamite. They returned with more than was needed.

"Alva sent word out last night that all hands are to be at Burnett's no later than seven o'clock," Roberts advised Hamlin. "They're goin' to gather here first and ride over to Box Elder together."

"That'll be all right. Have you fellows talked over what you're going to need tonight?"

"I'll get shovels and other tools laid out this afternoon," Buck told him. "It takes some time for dirt and rock fill to settle. I don't believe we'll have any trouble gittin' deep enough into it to make the charges do a real job."

During the hot afternoon it was pitiful to Hamlin to see cattle come in for water and stand bewildered on the bank on finding the creek dry. They moved along to the deep holes and when they found one they waded in, quenching their thirst but bellowing protestingly, unable to understand what had happened.

It was after four when Carla and her mother got back from town. They said Broken Rock was buzzing over the fact that Jep Tark had been hailed into court and found in contempt.

"Judge Pringle fined him a hundred and fifty dollars and sentenced him to thirty days in the lock-up," Carla informed him, with evident pleasure. "But just as you thought, Pierce, Dan Fallon (Tark's lawyer) took an appeal and he went free on bail."

'That's the end of that!" Lockhart snorted disgustedly. "Tark doesn't have to worry about injunctions now; he's got his dam up; Black Tail is dry!"

"For a few hours," Hamlin prophesied.

With the coming of evening the basin men began to ride in. Price Pickens and Ben Southard were among the first. They were in a happier frame of mind than they had been in months. Hamlin and the Association had waged a successful battle for them and they came prepared to put up a fight for the Black Tail men. Though they had not been enlightened regarding the inner workings of the night's undertaking, they knew its ultimate purpose was the destruction of T Bar's dam. The little man from Ten Mile, notorious for his low boiling point, filled the air with his violent threats against Tark.

"By God, we oughta drown that old bastard in his lake before we let the water out!"

"Don't work yourself into a lather, Price," Hamlin cautioned. "Cool heads are what we need tonight."

The others, aware of the seriousness of what they were embarking on, had little or nothing to say. Hamlin and Lockhart exchanged a few words and the latter said: "Time to be movin'."

They began to file out of the Cross Keys yard. Hamlin and Lockhart were the last to leave. Carla and her mother came out to beg them to be careful.

"I know what you're doin' is necessary, Tom," said Mrs. Lockhart, a catch in her voice, "but don't take any foolish chances. Please, Tom!"

"It'll be all right, Hattie," he assured her. "We're fightin' for our lives. We'll have to take what comes and make the best of it."

Carla looked up at Hamlin. He nodded in response to the silent appeal in her troubled eyes and lingered for a word as her father rode away. "I'll keep him close to me."

Roberts and Buck had received their final instructions. They were to wait another hour before starting up Black Tail for the dam. Hamlin raised a hand to them as he hurried out of the yard to overtake the others.

The expected reinforcements were waiting at Frank Adams' ranch. Without any loss of time the whole party struck east for Box Elder and Wick Burnett's.

The long twilight was gone and night was at hand by the time all were gathered there. If Burnett noticed that Skip Roberts was not among those present he didn't mention it. Hamlin spoke with him briefly. It had occurred to the former that the Box Elder man could have arranged to lead them into a trap in the mountains. He had mentioned it to Adams, who knew the Buckskins better than Burnett, and the two of them had decided that it would be wise to ride up ahead with their guide.

"If you're ready, Wick, I guess we can start moving. You're sure you can show us the way?"

"I won't have any trouble," the other answered lightly. Considering the dangerous nature of the game he was playing he was singularly self-possessed.

They were in the mountains half an hour later. In the dense blackness of early evening they could see only a few yards. The deer trail they were following went over a hogback. When they came down on the far side, Burnett took a wrong turn, either by accident or design. Adams called a halt.

"We should have turned to the right back there a few yards, Burnett. There's no trail here."

"I could be mistaken, it's so damn dark in here, but I don't believe it," the other declared.

"Let's make sure," said Hamlin. "Suppose you go back, Frank, to where you think we went wrong. We'll have some moonlight before long."

Adams located the spot where they had turned off the trail. Burnett was apologetic. Hamlin decided it had been an honest mistake. They went on, Adams and he watching Burnett closely. Before long the moon was up. It made the going easier. They struck a long narrow canyon where the black shadows were made to order for an ambush. They filed through it without incident and came out on a high, broken plateau. Hamlin glanced at Adams. The latter nodded, signifying that he knew where they were. In the moonlight, they could see low, rounded hills ahead of them.

"When we get across here we'll be out of the mountains," said Burnett. "What's the time?"

Hamlin got out his watch. "A few minutes after nine."

"That's about what I figured. We'll hit Black Tail before ten."

He was as good as his word. Hamlin called the men around him.

"We're going to change our plans some," he informed them, his gravity commanding their complete attention. "The committee agreed with me that secrecy being so necessary nothing would be said till we got here. We're going to get the dam tonight, but not with our guns. Here it is."

In a hushed silence he acquainted them with the carefully guarded plan. Once the men knew, they could not restrain their enthusiasm. Burnett didn't know what to say. He saw that he had been used as a decoy. He wanted to curse them for their treachery, forgetting his own, but he didn't dare lest they tell him to his face that he was Tark's man. He realized his danger, and it wasn't only the Association men he had to fear; he had sold them out, but Jep Tark would never see it that way; he'd contend that it was he who had been doublecrossed.

The blond man caught Hamlin watching him. It convinced him that it would be madness to attempt to bolt and run in the hope of reaching the T Bar crew in time to warn them.

"You take the lead and we'll start moving down the creek, Wick," Hamlin said quietly, reading the other's thought. "We'll be right behind you. Don't make any mistakes now."

Burnett understood him perfectly. He wanted to kill Hamlin.

They had gone no more than half a mile when a rifle shot shattered the night's peacefulness. Hard on its heels came a spattering volley from a dozen or more guns. The invaders sought cover instantly. Quitting their saddles hurriedly, they rolled up against rocks and the carcasses of fallen trees and returned a hot counterfire. The night became hideous with the crashing of guns. Hamlin noticed that Tom Lockhart was having trouble working his rifle.

"What is it, Tom?" he demanded anxiously.

"That first blast put a slug in my left arm," the other answered grittily. "I'll be all right. You better have a look at Burnett."

The latter had dropped his gun and was down behind the trunk of a dead cottonwood. Hamlin bent over him. "Where did it get you?"

"Right there." Burnett took his blood-stained hand away from his shoulder.

Hamlin tried to examine the wound but he could not see too well in the moonlight filtering down through the trees. "It's bleeding some," he muttered. "There's nothing we can do right now. You just lie there."

The fighting continued, swelling in intensity for a few minutes at a time and then tapering off to a few scattered shouts, only to be renewed with angry violence. But it continued, and that was what Hamlin wanted. Dallas Wilcox crawled up beside him with word that Homer Knox, the Squaw Creek rancher, had been killed.

Hamlin nodded solemnly. Homer Knox was a good man, but it wasn't a time for words. Words wouldn't have helped.

When Skip and Buck Ross heard the thunder of the distant guns they were a quarter of a mile below the dam. They closed in on it at once. At two hundred yards they left their horses and proceeded on foot.

They were out in the open, with an occasional clump of sage the only cover they could find. They took advantage of it, moving ahead a few feet at a time. Minutes were precious, and finding themselves unopposed, they became bolder. As they closed in they were almost persuaded that they had the dam to themselves. They were mistaken. A gun blossomed red on the rim of the little canyon.

"I see him," Buck muttered.

"So do I," said Roberts. "There's nothin' to do but turn wolf and let him have it."

They fired together. The T Bar man went down. In a few minutes they began using their shovels and picks, working feverishly. Hamlin had warned them that they couldn't expect to have more than forty to fifty minutes. With that thought in mind to spur them on, they sank the holes deeper and deeper and finally began to place the charges. They knew if the dynamite loosened the fill that the pressure of the backed-up water would tear out the dam.

"I reckon that's it, Buck," Roberts jerked out, perspiration dropping from his face. "Light the fuses and we'll clear out."

With no thought of sleep Carla and her mother sat on the gallery of the Cross Keys house. From far across the basin the night wind out of the Buckskin Hills brought them the faint murmuring of gunfire. They knew what it meant. It tightened their throats and had the same effect on every other woman who was listening. Suddenly the dull thunder of the explosions brought them to their feet. Carla ran down to the bridge to watch the creek, knowing if the dam had gone out that water would soon be roaring down Black Tail.

She heard the water coming a full minute before she saw the foaming crest tearing down the dry creek bottom. It struck the bridge with such fury that she picked up her skirts and ran. For a few minutes she was sure the bridge would be swept away. The water rose until the planks were awash, but the bridge held. Ten minutes later the creek was no higher than it often was in late spring.

"Now if Dad is only safe—and Pierce!" she prayed.

The reverberations of the explosion were still rumbling through the hills when the basin men raised a mighty shout of triumph. Hamlin hoped it was not premature. He saw Pickens and others watching the creek as though expecting the flow to begin moving faster. He knew if the dam had gone out that the rush of the released water would have no effect this far up Black Tail. He told them so and warned them to brace themselves for a determined attack.

It came as soon as the T Bar forces recovered their wits. Infuriated at having been outsmarted, and with Strahorn to whip them on, they threw caution to the winds and charged until no more than fifty yards separated them from the concealed foe. That was as far as they could get. After holding their ground a few minutes, they dropped back suddenly and the crashing of their guns ceased.

"They've had enough!" Price Pickens yelled. "They're gittin' in the saddle and droppin' down the crick!"

The fight was over. The basin men picked up their wounded, in addition to Lockhart and Burnett, three others had been struck, and draped the body of Homer Knox over the saddle he would never use again. Slowly they filed through the hills to Box Elder and

Burnett's ranch. Hamlin addressed them when they had gathered in the yard.

"Frank and Dallas have volunteered to take Homer home and break the bad news to the family. That leaves us with five men who need the services of a doctor. Burnett and Willis will have to be put in a wagon and driven to Broken Rock; the others say they'll be able to ride in. It's after there o'clock. A couple of us will go in with them. If we get started now, we'll be in town early in the morning."

Lockhart was averse to going in. "I can have that slug dug out of me at home."

"You're going to town, Tom," Hamlin insisted. "With a doctor available we won't risk any buckshot surgery."

The two halfbreeds who worked for Burnett ran out a wagon and hitched a team. The wagon-bed was filled with hay and the two wounded men made as comfortable as possible for the long ride. Burnett spoke to Hamlin.

"Why are you bothering about me?" he growled weakly. "You know you'd like to see me in hell."

"That's where you belong," was the tall man's curt response.

Dawn overtook them before they reached the Squaw. They halted there briefly. Adams got Hamlin aside. He dreaded the errand he and Dallas Wilcox had ahead of them.

"I only hope it wasn't for nothin', Pierce. We don't know yet if there's water comin' down Black Tail. I want to know. I'll be over later in the day."

Hamlin went on ahead as they neared Cross Keys. A savage grunt of satisfaction escaped him as he beheld Black Tail flowing bank full. He went to the house at once and relieved Carla and her mother of their worst fears. They agreed with him that though the wound Tom had received was not so serious that he should go to town.

"What about Skip and Buck?" he asked.

"Oh, they got back hours ago," Carla informed him.

"Did they have any trouble?"

"None at all, according to Skip. But you know how he minimizes anything like that. They were fired on and had to kill a T Bar man."

He caught the note of reproof in her voice and saw her shake her head regretfully.

"Carla," he said bluntly, "I don't like killing any better than you, but there are times when there is no other way to get justice. Men like your father, and Frank and Alva didn't seek this trouble. One man, and one only, is responsible."

He told them about Homer Knox.

"Oh, no!" Mrs. Lockhart cried. "That's terrible!"

"It is, Mrs. Lockhart. We paid a high price to put water back in Black Tail—one man killed and five wounded. I imagine T Bar fared even worse. I wish I could tell you it means the fighting is over, but I can't. The men are fired up now. They've won a big victory and they're talking already about pushing Jep Tark back to where he was years ago. Tom and the others are coming now. Don't talk to him more than a minute or two. I understand there's only two doctors in Broken Rock. I'd like to get there before T Bar brings in its wounded."

He had been careful to avoid any mention of Wick Burnett, preferring to have that come from Carla's father.

It was eight o'clock when Hamlin sat down at the counter in the restaurant that he and Skip had patronized before. He had just ordered his breakfast when Lin Bible came in and sat down beside him. The sheriff wasn't there to eat.

"Pierce, you show up in the early hours of the mornin' with five wounded men and T Bar has just come in with as many more," he said heavily. "I reckon that calls for an explanation."

Hamlin nodded woodenly. "It can't be any secret by now that there was a big fight in the hills above the T Bar house last night. Haven't you questioned anyone?"

"No, I preferred to do my talkin' to you. Doctors git the first call, then the undertaker. Is he goin' to be needed in the basin today?"

"Homer Knox, Lin—"

"Homer, eh?" The sheriff removed his hat and ran his fingers through his white hair. "I don't like to hear that. Somebody was sure to get it. You go on talkin'."

"There's water coming down Black Tail again."

"So the dam was blown sky high! You wouldn't know how that happened or who was responsible?"

"I'm afraid my memory ain't that good, Lin," Hamlin said, poker-faced.

"Perhaps that's just as well," the sheriff grunted. "Perhaps it will be just as well if I don't know too much about it, though Tark can't turn to the court for help. He thumbed his nose at the law just once too often."

Hamlin was weary by the time he got back to Cross Keys. He slept for a few hours, preferring sleep to dinner. The afternoon was half gone when he awoke. He was alone. Rubbing the sleep out of his eyes, he lit a cigarette and lay there smoking, more relaxed than he had been in days. It was cool in the bunkhouse, a pleasant breeze blowing in from the west. Lying there he cast up his account with Jep Tark. He knew he had hurt him, how seriously remained to be seen. But he was resolved that this was far from the end of it. Just pushing him off range he had wrongfully appropriated wouldn't be enough; it would have to be something more personal than that.

After he had shaved and sluiced himself down with a bucket of cold water, he dressed and walked up to the house. Carla came out as he reached the gallery.

"He's sleeping," she said, Hamlin understanding that she was referring to her father. "Getting Dad to go to bed in the daytime was next to impossible."

"I'd imagine so," he smiled as they sat down. "He won't be able to use his arm much for a week to ten days, but I'm sure you won't be able to keep him cooped up in the house. I don't see Skip or the men around."

"They're up the creek having a look at the stock." Carla's young face grew serious. "Pierce, you were right about Wick, I understand; Dad told me how you had trapped him. It shakes my faith in men; I was so sure he was aboveboard with us."

"Don't apologize for having been taken in by him," Hamlin said charitably. "He almost had me fooled."

She was silent for a moment or two.

"What are you going to do about him, Pierce?"

"I don't know that it's necessary to do anything about him. He's of no further use to Tark nor to us. As I told Skip, there's only one thing about Burnett that interests me. What tempted him to play Tark's game? Skip thinks it was just money. I don't."

"But what else?"

Hamlin shook his head in a baffled way. "That's what I've asked myself a hundred times. I don't know why, but the thought keeps popping into my mind that it must have been Annette."

Carla smiled skeptically. "Don't you find that hard to believe, Pierce?"

"I do. But it's a fact that he came up here from Miles City. That's where she hails from. They could have been acquainted down there—"

"And she induced Wick to turn traitor—is that what you mean?"

"Well, if you're going to pin me down," he said, with a grave smile, "I suppose it is."

11

There wasn't a church in the basin, but one Sunday a month a minister came out from Broken Rock and services were held in the Black Tail schoolhouse. A short distance to the rear of the school a plot of ground had been fenced off for a cemetery. Over the years a dozen or more people had been buried there, most of them young children, according to the legends on the headboards. There Homer Knox was laid to rest, with the Reverend Dickinson leading the mourners to the grave.

A big crowd had turned out. After the services, the women gathered about Mrs. Knox and drew off to themselves. The men clustered about the schoolhouse steps. Tom Lockhart, his arm in a sling, was one of them. He and Frank Adams and Hamlin formed the center of the group. Price Pickens was present. According to him (he claimed to have got his information from the doctor who had been called to T Bar) Tark had lost three men killed and a half dozen wounded, one seriously.

"That's why we ain't heard nothin' from him for a couple of days," he declared. "The old wolf's lickin' his wounds. Alva, if you and Titus and Wilkins mean to run him off the range he stole from you fellas, now is the time to do it; don't wait till he brings in new men.

All that part of the basin clear up to the dam used to be yores."

The enthusiasm that greeted the suggestion came as no surprise to Hamlin, nor could he disagree with the argument that with T Bar temporarily crippled they would never have a better opportunity to drive Tark out of the heart of the basin. There was a lot of talk. He listened without expressing an opinion. It quickly became apparent that what they proposed to do was to organize a drive similar to the one up Ten Mile and push T Bar cattle off the disputed range by force.

"They may put up a fight, but they can't stop us," Alva Williams asserted. "We got a few men put out of action. Overall it don't amount to anything; we got T Bar outnumbered five to one." He turned to Hamlin. "We ain't heard a word out of you, Pierce. What do you think?"

"When we organized it was the understanding that we'd go all the way," was Hamlin's carefully considered answer. "We certainly are not going to stop where we are and be satisfied with half a loaf. Before Tark started grabbing range he didn't have anything below the site of the dam. There's no question in my mind about going all out to push him back. I also agree with you that the time to do it is now. I differ with you, however, about how to go about it."

It took them by surprise. In one voice, half a dozen demanded an explanation.

"In the past we've always led from weakness," he told them; "we've always been the underdogs. We can lead from strength this time, and we can show Tark how strong we are by ordering him to move his stock off that range. We'll give him twenty-four hours to do it. If he fails, we'll tear into his stuff and run it out."

They stared at him incredulously. In a very small

voice Price Pickens said: "Honest to God, Pierce, you don't think he'd pay any attention to that, do you?"

"He just might, Price, if it doesn't give him a stroke, upstarts like us telling him where to head in." Hamlin's tone was briefly facetious, only to turn sober quickly. "He'll do one of two things: he'll either move his stuff or put up a shooting fight to keep it where it is."

"There may be some advantage in playin' it your way," Tom Lockhart conceded. "At least we'll have nothin' to lose. Of course there's nothin' to keep him from openin' his money bag and buyin' some land, same as you've done."

"That's something we can do too, Tom. But we can't buy all of it, neither can he; there's too much of it. I don't believe we have to worry about that. The thing for us to do is to serve notice on him yet this afternoon that we're giving him just twenty-four hours to clear out."

"How are we goin' to deliver the message?" Frank Adams inquired.

"Half a dozen of us will ride up the creek till we spot a T Bar man. We'll signal for a parley and I'll pass the word to him."

They wanted action, and they were getting it. Hamlin selected the men who were to accompany him. Lockhart offered to go, but to no avail.

"There's no point in the rest of you remaining here," Hamlin told the others, as he and his group were ready to ride. "Keep yourselves available tomorrow. If you're needed, you'll be told when and where to meet."

Skip stayed close to him as they moved up the basin. He had nothing to say, but the troubled look in his puckered eyes spoke for him. Hamlin thought to wait him out, knowing the Texan had something on his mind.

"Well, what is it?" he snapped, his patience exhausted.

"Just this; no T Bar rider is goin' to let this bunch git closer than a couple hundred yards of him; we'll have to pull up and you'll go on alone."

"That's right."

"Mister, you want to be damned sure he understands that your intentions are peaceable before you move up to him! There's been a lot of lead thrown in this basin the past few days. I wouldn't let no stranger ride up to me unless I knew his business. Neither would you. How you goin' to show him you ain't hostile?"

"When you fellows pull up, I'll hand you my gun and go in with my hands raised. That ought to be enough."

"You can't do more'n that," Roberts grumbled in agreement. "He may decide to run at the last minute. If he does, he'll throw a shot or two at you before he hightails it. You'll be a sittin' duck, Pierce."

"I know it," Hamlin acknowledged thinly. "I'll have to risk it. You watch Pickens. If he reaches for his gun, you stop him. He's the only one in the bunch who may lose his head."

Roberts nodded. "I'll keep an eye on him."

They had been among T Bar cattle for some time, little bunches grazing everywhere, without catching sight of a Tark rider. Turning west from the creek, they climbed a low ridge and from the crest saw two horsemen regarding them with interest. The pair were out on the flats a short distance from the ridge. Their attitude said they had no intention of running, though they were outnumbered three to one.

The bigger of the two had a rifle in his saddle boot. He yanked it out. Resting it across the horn of his saddle, he sat there waiting. Price Pickens was first to recognize him.

"The big fella is Joe Strahorn," he announced. "He's ugly; you watch yoreself, Hamlin."

"You do the same and keep your shirt on," the other advised bluntly. Speaking to all, he said: "We're skylined here; they can see every move we make. I'm going to hand Skip my gun now and go on alone."

He flung up his right hand, the accepted range sign for a parley, and went down the slope. At the bottom, he raised both hands and went on that way, guiding his horse with his knees.

"Stop where you are and state your business!" Strahorn called out when no more than fifty yards separated them.

"I got a message for Tark," Hamlin answered.

"All right, let's have it. I can hear you from there. Put your hands down and be damned careful what you do with 'em!"

The T Bar foreman stiffened as he listened to what Hamlin had to say. He couldn't credit his ears.

"By God, you got a crust, Hamlin, comin' up here to tell us to git off! I'll give the boss your message, all right, but I'm tellin' you to your teeth that we've taken all the pushin' around from you and your two-bit crowd that we're goin' to take!" A bullet had grazed his head in the fight on Black Tail. He wore a bandage that peeped out beneath his hat. "You're askin' for a showdown, and you'll sure git it! You turn your bronc now and git out of here."

Hamlin jogged back to the ridge. Skip's watchfulness had prevented Pickens from slapping a shot at the T Bar men to speed them on their way. But he was boiling.

"I saw him sassin' you, Hamlin," he growled. "I repeat what I said this afternoon; nuthin' will come of this. It was jest a waste of time."

He was mistaken. It was to have results that none of them foresaw. It brought Strahorn to Cross Keys early in the morning to see Lockhart.

"Jep wants to have a talk with you and Adams and Alva Williams," said he. "You can come to T Bar or he'll meet you at the school house this noon. The three of you are to come alone, and so will he. He says he won't stand for Hamlin bein' present."

Tark's offer to confer with the Association committee took both Lockhart and Hamlin by surprise.

"Pierce is runnin' things for us," the former protested. "We ain't havin' no meetin' without him bein' there to hear what's said."

"Then there won't be no meetin'," said Strahorn. "The old man won't have nothin' to do with Hamlin."

"Tom, I don't know that anything will come of talking to Tark, but I'd meet him at the schoolhouse if I were you. It'll be all right with me. You can get word to Frank in time and pick up Alva on your way up. I know the three of you won't be budged from the stand we've taken all along that we'll fight till T Bar is driven out of the middle and lower basin."

He took Lockhart aside. After several minutes of heated argument Lockhart was won over.

"All right," he told Strahorn, "you tell Tark the three of us will meet him at the Black Tail schoolhouse this noon."

"What do you think it means, Pierce?" Carla asked as she sat on the gallery with Hamlin and Skip after her father and Adams left.

"I don't know," he answered haltingly. "I would presume that Tark is going to offer us some sort of compromise that won't be acceptable to me."

"If you feel that way about it, why did you urge Tom to meet him?" Skip drawled provocatively.

"I thought it worthwhile to hear what Tark had to say. It's some satisfaction to me to have him rule me out. I guess he knows by now that the kid he used to slap around is responsible for his troubles."

The bitterness that she saw in his face frightened Carla. She realized that the one thing he didn't want was for her father and the basin men to enter into any sort of compromise with Jep Tark; he wanted the fight to continue until Tark was crushed. She could appreciate the deep sense of wrong that was responsible for the vengeance that ruled him. Her sympathy went out to help him, but in her heart she knew that what she wanted above all was peace, with a fair measure of justice, and an end to the shooting and killing.

Lockhart and Adams returned earlier than Hamlin expected. He was down at the barn with Skip, watching Buck Ross shoe a horse when the two men rode in.

"Well, what did he have to say?" Hamlin asked at once.

"He made us quite a proposition," Lockhart answered. "He is willing to draw a deadline across the basin, running from the southern tip of the Blue Flats to the ridge where the dam stood and on west to Ten Mile valley. He's ready to agree to pull all his stuff in back of that line and we're to have everythin' this side of it. That's some concession, Pierce."

"It certainly is," Hamlin said coolly.

"We hurt him worse than we figgered for him to agree to anything like this," Adams spoke up. "It gives us everythin' we was fightin' for."

"It doesn't give me what I was fighting for," Hamlin returned, his lips thinning angrily. "If Tark's been taking a licking, the credit belongs to me. I stopped him on the Blue Flats and over on Ten Mile. There's been a few other things I can recall. We had an understanding; we were to stick together. When you found you could get what you wanted you didn't hesitate to sell me down the river."

"How can you say that?" Lockhart cried indignantly. "We wouldn't have got anywhere without you. We appreciate all you've done for us, Pierce."

"There's no question about that," came from Adams.

"That's fine!" Hamlin observed with cutting sarcasm. "I imagine Alva Williams is just as eager to agree to this proposition as you."

"Naturally he is—and why not?" Adams demanded gruffly, irked by the other's attitude. "He stands to git back about three thousand acres of fairly good range."

"Get it back for how long? I figured the two of you had too much sense to fall for a deal like this."

"Pierce, let's not have any hard words," Lockhart protested. "Nothin's been decided; it'll have to be put to a vote."

"No, Tom, it's all decided right now; there won't be a vote against it. Not one! The three of you will have to hold yourselves responsible for what follows. When Tark dangled his bait in front of your eyes you didn't hesitate a minute about selling me out. Before he gets through with you you'll find that you've sold yourselves out too."

He wasn't finished. Controlling his voice, he continued.

"If you think Tark made this proposition because he's so badly licked that he had to find a way out, you're fooling yourselves. You've missed the whole point of it. This thing was aimed at me and at nobody else; he figured if he offered you a deal like this that you'd snap it up and walk out on me. That was what he wanted. He knew you better than I did."

"See here, Hamlin," Adams whipped out resentfully, "I don't like to be told to my face that I'm a goddam fool!"

"No one does, Frank. No one likes to be played for one; but I was this time. Back in the beginning someone said, I think it was Price Pickens, that my game was to use you men to pull my own chestnuts out of the fire. That wasn't my idea. Maybe it should have been; it would have prepared me for this. Every time we pulled off a successful move, I thought I was helping myself as well as you. That was my mistake; I'm back where I started. But I've still got a considerable stake in the basin. I swore I'd pull Tark down, and I ain't changing my mind about that."

"Pierce, you know we'll help you any way we can," Lockhart said, distressed by the turn things had taken.

"No, Tom! That cunning old bastard outsmarted me this once. He won't do it a second time; I'll play my own hand the rest of the way."

He walked away. Skip followed him to the bunkhouse and sat down with him. He understood as well as Hamlin that they couldn't remain at Cross Keys. A brooding silence descended on them. Hamlin broke it.

"Tark must be having a good laugh at my expense!" His face was hard and flat. "A deadline won't mean anything to him. He'll respect it just long enough to be sure he's moved me out of the picture, then he'll begin crowding them back again." He shook his head dejectedly. "What we've done may have annoyed him a little, but it hasn't accomplished a thing. He can sit up there on T Bar and thumb his nose at me."

"Don't take it so hard," Skip advised. "Tark put

over a fast one on you, but he ain't thumbin' his nose at anybody, not after the pastin' he's been takin'."

Hamlin stared at him piercingly for a whole minute.

"Skip, did it ever occur to you that they'd dump me this way?"

"No, but there's somethin' to be said for the stand they're takin'. You can't expect men to go on fightin' when they can't see that they've got anythin' left to fight for. Oh, I know this deadline business is a trick; it ain't goin' to settle anythin', at least not for long. Tark may hold off till after the fall shippin's over, then, as you said, he'll start movin' in on 'em."

"You couldn't make the damned fools believe it if you talked yourself blue in the face!" Hamlin exploded. "I ain't interested in waiting to hear how they vote; we're through here, Skip. The thing for us to do is gather up our gear and pull out. We'll go to Broken Rock and live at the hotel until I can figure out what to do."

Roberts nodded. "It won't take us long to throw our stuff together." He wasn't happy about it. "I reckon Tom Lockhart feels as bad about this as you do, Pierce. I'd hate to see you hold a grudge against him. And there's Carla—she's goin' to be awful cut up over your leavin'. She thinks a heap of you."

Hamlin's jaws came together with an audible click as he got to his feet, a desperate look in his eyes.

"Good God, Skip, do you think it's going to be easy for me to tell her I'm leaving? I won't lie to you; she means a lot to me. But I can't expect her to take my side against her father. That's why I want to get it over with quickly. I'll pick up our few things if you'll catch up our horses. We'll stop at the house for a minute before we pull out. If I can get Tom to say how much we owe him for our keep, I'll pay him."

"He won't take a cent, Pierce."

"I don't suppose he will."

Roberts had been gone only a minute or two when Carla Lockhart ran up to the open door of the bunkhouse.

"Pierce, what are you doing?" she cried, her voice tremulous with excitement.

"We've leaving for town," he said haltingly. "I was going to stop at the house before I left."

"Pierce Hamlin, you come out here! I want to talk to you!"

He came to the door, looking down at her and not trusting himself to speak.

"Pierce, you're being very, very foolish!" she said tensely. She was both frightened and angry. "Is it your pride that's been hurt, or are you so consumed with hatred for Jep Tark that nothing else matters?"

"Loyalty matters to me. I was sure I could count on it from your father and Adams; I wasn't so sure about Alva Williams. When they had a chance to prove it they let me down."

"That's awfully unfair of you," she burst out, her voice sliding off key. "Dad never had any thought of letting you down, as you put it, and I'm sure Frank Adams didn't. They know that but for you Jep Tark wouldn't have tossed them as much as a bone."

"Well, a bone is all he's offering them, and they won't find any meat on it," he informed her, his tone sharp and biting. "Don't you get the idea that this is the hour of deliverance; it's just a respite, and it'll be damned brief!"

Her eyes flashed hotly. "It was all intended, I understand, just to slap you down!" Her withering sarcasm made him tremble. "I doubt it, but if it were true, I would expect you to fight back instead of running."

It stung him and he answered with a low mocking laugh.

"I'm not running very far, Carla. And you can be sure I'll go on fighting. I didn't come back to Montana to quit now. When Skip and I came here it was on the understanding that we could pay for our keep. I want to take care of that obligation before I leave."

"Pierce, you've hurt Dad enough without humiliating him further by offering him money. Don't stop at the house, just go. Please, for my sake!" she pleaded.

"Very well, if that's how you want it," he said huskily.

All his anger ran out of him as he gazed at her, so young, so lovely and so desirable. She was crying softly. He wanted to take her in his arms and tell her he loved her; that there never could be anyone else for him.

"Good bye—" she whispered, her heart in her eyes.

She was gone then. Skip and Buck Ross found him standing there, lost in wonder.

12

It was evening when Lin Bible wandered into the office of the Yellowstone House and glanced casually at the register. A little grunt of unexplained surprise escaped him as he caught Hamlin's name and Skip's.

"Chub, are these fellas goin' to be with you jest overnight?" he asked the clerk.

"No, Hamlin said they'd be with us some time."

The sheriff glanced into the bar, looking for them. They were not there or out on the porch. He came down the steps and was looking up and down the street when he saw them coming.

"I jest saw your names on the register," he told them. "Chub says you expect to be in town for some time. What's the idea?"

Hamlin smiled at the unconsciously irascible note in the sheriff's tone.

"You sound as though you were prepared to disagree with it whatever it is," he said lightly. "Suppose we sit down on the porch and I'll tell you."

Bible's scowl darkened as he listened to Hamlin's account of his break with the basin men and why he had left Cross Keys.

"I suppose you're going to tell me I acted too hastily, Lin."

The old man shook his head. "No—no, I'm not

goin' to say that; I'm jest sorry it had to happen that way. I can understand their reasonin' and I can understand yours. They were fightin' for one thing and you for another. They knew that. After all you did for 'em, they shouldn't have made any deal with Tark. I agree with you it was a damned smart move he made."

"You agree that it was aimed at me?"

"What else? Tark ain't ready to be run out of the basin. He ain't pretending to give up seven, eight thousand acres of range unless he's got an ax to grind." The sheriff shook his head again. "What are you goin' to do now?"

"I don't know. There must be some way to get at him. Have you heard any more about that contempt action?"

"No, Fallon will drag it out. Jep will have to pay his fine, but the jail sentence will be held excessive and be thrown out. At least that's my guess."

"Is Burnett still in town?" Skip inquired.

"No, Doc Squires patched him up. He went back to Box Elder a couple of days ago. Did you see the ad he put in the *Monitor*?"

"No—"

"He's put his ranch up for sale. He'll have a hard time sellin' it, beef prices droppin' and money purty tight. It's a nice little spread, but he ain't got much on it. Three hundred head he claims."

"What is it worth, Lin?" asked Hamlin.

"He's askin' eighteen thousand. I'd say a fair price would be fifteen to sixteen. The bank's got a big plaster on it." He gave Hamlin a sharp, unexpected glance. "You ain't interested?"

"No, just curious."

Several days passed, interminable days for Hamlin.

Though he racked his brain trying to find a crack in Jep Tark's armor, he failed to hit on anything that he could consider seriously. Skip suffered with him, but could not help.

"It's beginnin' to look like you're up against a stone wall," he sympathized.

"I'm not ready to believe that, Skip; something will turn up."

He knew the Association had accepted Tark's offer without a dissenting vote. It meant nothing to him. He spent hours on the hotel porch, thinking and watching the life of the town. If he wasn't there he could usually be found at the sheriff's office. He and Skip were on the porch early one morning when they saw Tark drive in with Annette. After passing the hotel they turned the next corner in the direction of the depot. It wasn't long before they heard the westbound train for Miles City and points beyond blowing for Broken Rock. Annette came back alone and had her breakfast at the hotel.

"I reckon we can figger that out," Skip drawled. "The old man's goin' down the line on business."

"To hire new hands in Miles City, no doubt," Hamlin observed. "Let's go in and eat. We'll get a good look at this dame at the same time."

Annette caught their attention focused on her. She returned it with a scornful glance.

"She knows who we are, Skip. What do you think of her?"

"Just a cute little bitch, hard as nails," was the Texan's brutally realistic appraisal. "But not too smart."

"Why do you say that?"

"She ain't been able to get her fingers on old Tark's bankroll or she'd be long gone. I've known a hundred of her kind: they're all alike, just alley cats."

"He knew what she was and is," Hamlin interposed. "It hasn't kept him from being crazy about her."

"I'll grant you he is," Skip argued, "but don't tell me she's crazy about him. She ain't stickin' with that old goat because she likes his company. If he wasn't scared of losin' her he'd have taken her along to Miles City this mornin'. He wasn't takin' any chances."

Annette finished her breakfast before they did. Passing their table on her way out of the dining room she said under her breath: "I hope you crumbs had a good time talking me over!"

They could see her out at the desk paying her check. Skip grinned shamelessly. "I'm glad I don't have to dance to that little hellcat's tune. It almost makes me feel sorry for old Tark."

Hamlin wasn't listening. This chance meeting with Annette had started a train of thought in his mind that fascinated him.

"What is it?" Skip demanded when the other's long silence became unendurable.

"You can call it a hunch or whatever you please," was Hamlin's sober answer, "but I believe I can reach Tark through her, hurt him as nothing else would hurt him. It was always your idea that Wick Burnett was acting as Tark's spy just for money. I never thought so. I don't believe I ever mentioned it to you, but when I learned that he was from Miles City and she was too, I wondered if what he was doing was on her account; if she was the go-between. We were going to watch Burnett, but we never got around to doing it. We got the time for it now and I'm going to."

"I'm afraid that doesn't make much sense to me," the Texan demurred. "Burnett's trying to sell and get out of this country. That doesn't sound like there's anythin' between him and Annette. You don't even know they're acquainted."

"I don't," Hamlin acknowledged, "but I mean to find out. I'm going to be better acquainted with both of them before I'll admit that I've gone off on a trail that doesn't lead anywhere.

It seemed logical to begin his quest for information with the sheriff. He realized, however, that the nature of his questions would at once disclose their purpose to Lin.

"That'll be all right," he reflected. "I can be frank with him; I know it won't go any further."

The sheriff was out of town for the day. Hamlin was waiting for him when he returned in the late afternoon. Lin sat down heavily and reached for his pipe.

"It's been a hot day and I feel a little beat," he grumbled. "I had to go north of the river to serve some papers in a lawsuit. I didn't mind the ten-mile ride up to Basin, but I lost a lot of time ferryin' acrost and another hour when I got back. It was three o'clock by then, and I hadn't had any dinner. Beauchamp said he'd have his squaw cook me somethin'." The sheriff made a wry face. "I wish to God she hadn't; I can still taste the greasy stuff."

Basin was just a flag stop on the Northern Pacific, ten miles northeast of Broken Rock. As Hamlin remembered it there was nothing there but the shipping pens and a hand-operated signal which only the east and westbound local trains honored. On the Yellowstone, three miles to the north, there was a chain ferry. Hamlin surmised that Beauchamp was the current ferryman.

"What have you been doin', Pierce?"

"Nothing much. I been waiting to ask you a couple of questions."

"Wal, fire away."

Though they were alone Hamlin unconsciously hitched his chair a little nearer the desk.

"Lin, has anything ever given you reason to believe that Annette Tark and Burnett were acquainted before they came up here?"

"Why, no!" the sheriff answered, plainly, taken aback by the question. "Hell, I don't know they're even acquainted now. What are you drivin' at?"

"Just this: you know Burnett turned informer for Tark. Why? He surely knew the danger he was running. It couldn't have been for the money he got out of it."

"Why not?"

"Because Tark wouldn't have offered him enough to make it worth his while. But if money was the reason, will you tell me what gave Tark the idea that Burnett could be bought?"

It was only a rhetorical question. Hamlin didn't expect an answer. He went on.

"It would have been a simple matter if Annette was acquainted with Burnett and suggested to the old man that she could arrange it."

"Humph!" Lin Bible grunted. "I see what you mean. You're beginnin' to make sense. Do you know anythin' to back it up or is this jest a hunch?"

"Just a hunch, Lin. I don't know a thing, but I'm going to put two and two together and find out if it adds up to four. If it does I'll go on from there. There must be at least a couple of people in town who moved up here from Miles City and might have known Burnett and Annette down there."

"We've often had a man or two from Miles City

workin' here in town. There was a fella by the name of Jack Rusk, a bartender who worked in the Gem for a time. He's been gone a year or more. I swear I can't name anyone else. I—" He checked himself abruptly. "Say, I know one! That no-account Frenchman who runs the ferry is a Miles City man."

"What's his name?"

"Beauchamp—Bat Beauchamp. He's the sort of character who may be able to tell you what you want to know. He was in trouble three or four times before he was run out of Miles City, peddlin' whisky to Injuns and doin' a little rustlin'. I ain't had no trouble with him, but I suspect he's sellin' whisky at the ferry. Go see him tomorrow and let me know how you make out."

"Do you think he'll talk, Lin?"

"I don't know. He's cagey. You tell him I sent you to see him. That may open him up."

Purposely getting a late start so as not to arrive at the ferry until the morning was well along, Hamlin and Roberts rode out of Broken Rock and followed the little-used road that paralleled the railroad for several miles before it ended. They took to the tracks then until they struck the road out of Yellowstone Basin. It brought them to the flag stop.

It was a desolate spot, just a siding and the weather-beaten shipping pens. For a few days a year there was activity there, most of the beef that left the basin being shipped from that point. They went on and reached the river and Beauchamp's cabin thirty minutes later.

Beauchamp came out as they rode up. He was an obese, loose-tissued man with a pendulous mouth and a ragged, drooping mustache. He was neither friendly nor unfriendly.

"You want to cross?" he asked.

"No, we want to have a talk with you. Lin Bible sent us out."

Beauchamp withdrew noticeably into his flabby shell.

"Dis got somet'ing to do wit de law?" he inquired, darkly suspicious.

"No, this is strictly personal, Bat. When you were hanging out around Miles City how well did you know Wick Burnett?" The question was framed that way in the hope it might trip him and it was successful.

"I nevaire know heem too good," Beauchamp replied, when his natural instinct would have been to deny knowing the man at all. He realized his slip a moment after he made it. Trying to cover it, he said guilefully: "Big swells don't have no time for poor falla like Bat Beauchamp."

"At least you'd heard of him?"

"*Oui—*" was the guarded answer.

"What was his business, Bat?"

The Frenchman shrugged. "Why you not ask heem? He's got ranch on Box Elder crick."

Hamlin produced a twenty-dollar goldpiece and offered it to him. "Will you answer my question now?"

Beauchamp had a long look at the coin. "He was best faro dealer in town. He ran hees own game in de Silver Palace."

"Who was his girl?"

"He have plentay girl, I guess." Bat laughed obscenely.

"Was one of them Annette Davis?"

The Frenchman's little start of surprise told Hamlin that he had struck pay dirt.

Beauchamp shook his head. "I dunno. I don't keep track of hees girl."

Hamlin pretended to believe him and did not press the point. He was satisfied that he had established a connection between Annette and Burnett. He thought it wise to put some other questions to Beauchamp, all irrelevant as far as he was concerned but designed to confuse the Frenchman as to the reason for his interest in Burnett. Since the latter shipped from Basin he undoubtedly had some contact with Beauchamp, however limited.

"We'll see you again, Bat," said he. "If I can find a bargain I intend to buy a spread. I'll be shipping from Basin."

This was just a little artistic deception, born of the moment; he had no interest in buying a ranch in Yellowstone Basin. He and Roberts rode away. The latter was prompt with a question.

"Are you sure he was lyin' about not knowin' the woman?"

"Of course he was! He knows Annette was Burnett's girl."

"Then he must know she's Tark's wife."

"Certainly! He may not know who I am, but chances are he does. The sooner we get off this road after we cross the N. P. the better. If we're careful we ought to be able to get into the mountains without being seen."

They had left Broken Rock outfitted to spend a day or two in the Buckskins and keep a close watch on Burnett and his Box Elder ranch. They encountered no one. Late in the afternoon, from a rim high above the basin, they were in position to look down on the house and with the aid of Hamlin's binoculars watch what went on there. They caught frequent glimpses of Burnett as he moved about the ranch yard. He appeared to be there alone. Toward evening his two Sioux half-breeds rode in. He spoke to them at length. Afterwards they herded his small bunch of horses down to the creek to water.

"Everythin' seems normal down there," Skip drawled. He was tired and hungry. "He ain't goin' nowheres and he ain't havin' any visitors."

Hamlin could not do less than agree with him. They remained where they were, however, until night was at hand. They moved back into the mountains then, cooked their supper and relaxed.

"We may have better luck tomorrow," Hamlin remarked. "If he leaves the ranch we'll try to follow him. God knows with the feeling there is against him he won't be off to do any visiting in the basin."

He had been told in town that Tark was pulling back his stock as he had agreed. He could imagine that spirits were running high among the basin men as a result. He wondered how things were at Cross Keys, especially with Carla. It was an awkward situation; he couldn't go to her and he knew she was too proud to come to him, but he refused to believe that he had lost her.

"If I mean half as much to her as she does to me, this isn't the end of everything between us," he told himself. It couldn't be. When the mission that had brought him home to Montana was accomplished he'd be free to prove his devotion to her.

He drifted off to sleep and she wandered through his dreams. Skip was frying bacon when he opened his eyes. "Smells good," he yawned.

"Come on, Pierce, roll out of your blanket; the coffee's boilin'."

The Box Elder ranch was not yet astir when they returned to their perch on the rim. Soon after, however, the two halfbreeds emerged from the kitchen and went down to the corral to saddle their broncs.

"Been in to breakfast," Skip averred.

The two men jogged out of the yard, one went up

the creek, the other down, obviously for no other purpose than to make a routine check of Burnett's scattered cattle. Burnett came out of the house some time later with a fishing rod in his hand. Walking over to the creek, he began casting for trout.

Hamlin and Roberts watched him catch a dozen. He cleaned the fish on the creek bank and then sauntered back to the house.

"He don't seem to have anythin' on his mind," Skip complained.

"It doesn't look like it," Hamlin conceded.

The two halfbreed riders returned and busied themselves for the rest of the morning with routine ranch chores. Burnett called them to the house at noon. Shortly after dinner they saddled a horse for him and left it at the hitch rack by the kitchen door. Burnett came out a few minutes later and rode away at once, striking across his own range and down Box Elder. The easy pace at which he rode suggested that he was going a long piece. .

"He's either going to town, which wouldn't interest me, or answering a summons from Beauchamp to come to the ferry."

"If we're goin' to tail him, Pierce, we better git movin'," Skip advised.

"Not just yet. We can follow him with the glasses for a couple of miles if he takes the Broken Rock road. If we lose sight of him it'll sure look like he's headed for Beauchamp's cabin. I'd like to catch him there."

The Broken Rock road ran through a succession of little valleys that had some scrub timber. Burnett would disappear briefly and then reappear. That pattern was broken abruptly; they saw him fade from view as he rode slowly into a pass between some low hills.

They expected him to emerge a little further on. They waited, but no more was to be seen of him.

"What do you make of that?" Skip asked querulously. "Looks like he's given us the slip."

"I wouldn't say that; he didn't know he was being watched. He may be sticking to the road. It could make a turn to the north through those hills; I'm not familiar enough with it to say one way or the other. If he's on his way to town, which he likely is, there's no reason why we should try to catch up with him. Let him go. If he's making for Beauchamp's we can get there almost as soon as he does. Let's go!"

It was a little after three when they came in sight of the ferry. Beauchamp was on his way across the river. He had two passengers and their horses. Hamlin put the glasses on them. Neither was Wick Burnett.

"Don't see a horse tethered around the cabin," Skip remarked. "Don't look like Burnett is here."

"I'm afraid not. He's in town by now, no doubt. We'll wait till Bat gets back and give him another song and dance."

They rode up to the cabin. Beauchamp's Indian woman came out. She was a River Crow, fat and dirty. They attempted to question her, but she gestured that she neither spoke nor understood English.

The Frenchman was half an hour getting back. Though they made no further reference to Burnett, Beauchamp was not taken in by their apparent friendliness. After wasting a few minutes with him they set out for town.

They were in the hotel barn, putting up their horses, a little before six o'clock when Lin Bible came hurrying down the alley that led back to the barns. As a rule he never betrayed any signs of excitement no matter what was on his mind. That wasn't the case this evening.

"I saw you fellas ride in," he said at once. "I'm tellin' you there's hell to pay. Jep got back from Miles City on the afternoon train. Annette was in town to meet him. He stopped at the bank and drew out some money—a thousand dollars he says. They started home. About three miles out of town they was held up by a masked man. He clubbed Tark with his pistol—it took fourteen stitches to sew up his scalp—and got away with the money."

"What time was that?" Hamlin inquired, vaguely uneasy.

"About half-past three. Tark says he recognized the man's voice. He claims it was you."

Hamlin was momentarily stunned. "Lin," he demanded gravely, "do you believe it?"

"Hell, no! Of course I don't. But we got to prove it wasn't you."

"That ought to be easy. We were at the ferry, talking with Bat Beauchamp, fifteen miles away, at the time of the holdup."

"Thank God you were!" the sheriff snorted wrathfully. "Tark was held up, sure enough, and his money taken, but tryin' to fasten the job on you is just a slimy attempt to salvage somethin' out of it."

"Lin," Skip Roberts said with manifest anxiety, "that Beauchamp is as slippery as an eel. Is there a chance he'll deny talkin' with us this afternoon?"

The sheriff pulled down the corners of his mouth in a fearsome grimace. "He'll talk! I'll see to that! It's all the alibi you need, Pierce. You boys come with me now; we'll go around the corner to Doc Squires' place. He's got Tark in bed. We'll find out if Jep's jest bluffin' or means business!"

13

Squires was in the office of his little cottage hospital when they walked in.

"Doc, can we see Jep? I want to question him a bit," said Lin.

"Sure. His wife's in the bedroom with him."

Annette was seated beside the bed. The old man was holding her hand. To Hamlin's eyes she looked bored to death. She straightened up and her face paled with an obscure anxiety as she caught sight of the sheriff.

Tark glowered at his visitors and let them feel his hatred.

"You folks have had some time to think things over," Bible observed, his tone cold and hostile. "Are you still of the opinion that this man (he indicated Hamlin) is the one who held you up?"

"I didn't say that," Annette snapped. "I said the man was tall, that's all."

"Lots of tall men in this country," Lin reminded her. "Now you, Jep, you said before witnesses that you recognized Hamlin by his voice. That gives him grounds for legal action against you unless you can prove it."

"I'll prove it!" Tark snapped. "You lock him up!"

"I'll take him into custody when a charge has been filed against him and you've signed a warrant," was the sheriff's flinty response. "You won't do that. And this ain't jest a case of your bein' mistaken. You know you're lyin'. You haven't exchanged fifty words with Pierce since he came back. How would you recognize his voice? This is jest a·dirty, foul attempt to smear him."

Tark reared up in bed and shook his fist at him.

"Damn your hide, Bible, you can stand up for him all you please; it don't make no difference to me!" he sputtered. "Before I'm through I'll show you who's lyin'!"

"You old fool, I got you up a tree and I'll prove it right now," Lin jeered. "The robbery took place about half-past three. Pierce was fifteen miles away, talkin' to Bat Beauchamp at the chain ferry on the Yellowstone. Roberts here was with him. You ain't got a leg to stand on."

The master of T Bar could not repress a grunt of dismay at this unexpected disclosure. "I don't believe it!" he groaned, sinking back on the pillows. "Beauchamp's word don't count for nothin'."

"It'll count with a jury," the sheriff asserted grimly. "It was someone right here in town, or mebbe one of your imported gunslicks, who tapped you on the head and took your money. It sure was somebody who knew that with pay-day comin' up on T Bar you'd stop in at the bank when you got back from Miles City and have the money on you. I'll do what I can to run him down, but I'm afraid I won't git far."

Hamlin caught the sigh of relief that escaped Annette as they went out. When they reached the street, Lin said: "I don't believe you'll hear any more out of Tark about this, Pierce. But to play it safe I'll bring Bat in and have him give the D. A. a signed statement before Tark has a chance to git to him."

The sheriff was leaving them at the hotel when Hamlin called him back.

"Lin, who was in town from the basin this afternoon?"

"Not a soul. Ben Southard was in this mornin'."

Hamlin thanked him and he and Roberts went upstairs to their room.

"Well," Skip said, drawing the word out as dramatically as he could, "do you want to venture a guess as to who got Tark's money?"

"I wouldn't call it a guess," Hamlin answered, anger flushing his face. "That was just blind luck, going back to the ferry. Otherwise I'd have been in a tough spot even with Lin coming through for me. It's a scurvy trick not to tell him what we know about Burnett. But you get this straight, Skip: I ain't interested in tying Wick Burnett into the holdup."

"It was Burnett, wasn't it?"

"Certainly! We saw him leave his ranch. At the gait he was moving, he would have been within a couple of miles of town by three o'clock. This job was planned ahead of time. He picked out the spot he had chosen for the job and just waited for Tark and Annette to show up. You heard Lin say Burnett wasn't in Broken Rock this afternoon. And that's only the half of it."

"What do you mean?"

"Annette was in on the deal. She knew when Tark would be getting back. I'll go even further and say she knew he'd be drawing money for the ranch. All she had to do was slip the information to Burnett and leave the rest to him."

Hamlin was still boiling. He tore off his shirt and undershirt and sloshed water into a basin for a sponge-off.

"You know why she claims it was a tall man who stuck them up?"

"Because you couldn't call Burnett tall—"

"Exactly!"

Roberts just nodded and laid out his razor and fresh linen. As much to himself as to the other, he said: "Christ, he must be hard up—puttin' his ranch up for sale and pullin' off a robbery!"

"I don't figure it's so much a case of being hard up as them wanting to get their hands on some quick money," Hamlin declared as he toweled himself off.

Roberts laughed incredulously. "Oh, no, Pierce, you're drawin' the long bow now. I can believe Burnett would be interested in gittin' his hands on some cash, but when you drag Tark's wife into it, I can't see it. It don't make sense unless you got the idea they're gittin' ready to clear out. If that's it you're just whistlin' in the dark; you got no reason for thinkin' so."

"Not the slightest," Hamlin agreed. "But it's a fascinating idea," he added with an unholy chuckle. "It would just about knock Jep Tark off his rocker. The washstand is yours, Skip. Get cleaned up and we'll go downstairs. After two days of your cooking," he said facetiously, "I'll enjoy my supper."

The sheriff had Bat Beauchamp in town by noon. He hustled him to the county prosecutor's office and got a signed statement, made under oath, that established Hamlin's presence at the ferry at the time of the holdup and clearly demonstrated his innocence.

Tark left the doctor's that afternoon and returned to T Bar with Annette, and without going near the courthouse. Lin reported the facts to Hamlin with manifest satisfaction.

"I let him know we had Bat's signed statement. That stopped him. It leaves the way wide open for you to start suit against him for slander or defamation of character or whatever you want to call it. I believe you can collect damages."

"I won't bother with that," said Hamlin. "I'll find a way to hurt him worse than that."

He was still marking time several days later when he saw Tom Lockhart drive into town. Tom was alone. Hamlin couldn't help wondering if it was because Carla knew he was in Broken Rock, and wanting to avoid him, that she had not accompanied her father this morning. He met Lockhart on the street a bit later. The meeting was friendly, but not without some embarrassment on both sides.

"I'm mighty sorry we had to fall out the way we did, Pierce. Frank and I talk about it every time we meet. I don't blame you for condemnin' us. On the other hand, we'd been takin' it on the chin so long that when we saw a way out we forgot about you and grabbed it."

"There's no hard feelings on my part, Tom. You folks were fighting for one thing and I had something else in mind. How are things in the basin?"

"Pickens got us into trouble. He wasn't satisfied with gittin' back all he'd ever claimed; he had to push across the line for half a mile. Strahorn threw the whole T Bar crew at him. There was a fight. When it was over Price found himself back down below the Forks. I went up to T Bar yesterday and had a talk with Jep. To my surprise he ordered Strahorn to pull back to the line."

They talked it over for a minute or two.

"You know you're always welcome at Cross Keys, Pierce. The missus and Carla would like to see you."

"How is Carla?" Hamlin put the question hesitantly.

"Oh, she's fine I guess." Lockhart sounded anything

but certain about it. "I tried to git her to come in with me today, but she said no. She's been poutin' about somethin' ever since you left. I know she thinks we didn't treat you right. When I agree with her, she takes off in some other direction. They say never try to understand a woman. Reckon they're right."

Hamlin nodded. "I'm afraid so," he remarked for want of something better to say. "I'll be out one of these days."

They shook hands in parting. Just talking about Carla gave Pierce Hamlin a lift. Skip noticed it as they sat down to dinner.

"What's got you perked up, Pierce?"

"I ran into Tom Lockhart down the street. We had a friendly talk."

"About Carla?" the Texan inquired with a smile.

"Her name entered the conversation," Hamlin replied, shutting him off.

They were in the hotel barroom that evening when Joe Strahorn walked in. He was in a sullen mood. Things had not been going his way lately. Over the years his had been the actual job of pushing T Bar further and further down the basin, forcing other outfits off range they had been using, destroying fences when they stood in his way, resorting to gunfire when necessary and risking his life a hundred times over in the incessant strife that was born of T Bar's aggressions. To see everything below the so-called deadline, thousands of acres of range for which he had fought and bled, handed back, however temporarily, to the Association members was almost more than he could bear, and not only because he nursed a selfish interest in T Bar.

It explained the avidity with which he had attacked Price Pickens and thrown him back on his ear. To be ordered again to give up what he had won was the final straw. He blamed it all on Annette, justly or unjustly. In his eyes she had made old Jep a soft-headed weakling. He knew her secret, and though it would be no advantage to him to divulge it, to do so would hurt her, and that would be satisfaction enough. He fancied he knew who would make the most of it.

When Strahorn had had a drink or two he moved along the bar to where Hamlin and Skip stood. Others were present. Lowering his voice so as not to be overheard, he said: "This will surprise you, Hamlin. But don't git me wrong: Jep Tark is my boss and T Bar is my brand. But I can't take no more of that woman. I hate her guts. She goes ridin' in the hills most every afternoon. You follow her, see where she goes and who she meets. It'll tell you what you want to know. You watch Annette!"

That was all he had to say. Swinging his bulk around he trudged out.

"That musta surprised you, comin' from him," Roberts drawled.

"Yeh. Let's get out of here; I want to think it over."

They found they had the hotel porch to themselves. They had been seated there for several minutes before Hamlin spoke.

"We know more about Annette than he thinks we do. When she goes riding she meets Burnett, of course. Sounds like watching her will pay off better than watching him."

"You don't think this is a trick to get us in the hills and knock us off?"

"No, I believe Strahorn's on the level about this. She's been coming between him and the old man, so he's tossing her to the wolves. I'm going to take his tip. We'll get into the mountains the same way we went last time and drift south into the Buckskin Hills. You better get grub enough to last us three or four days. We'll stay out till we turn up something this trip."

"You want me to hire a pack horse?"

"I don't think that's necessary, Skip. If we have to dodge T Bar riders, and we may, a pack animal would slow us down."

They left town in the morning. Swinging around to the north of the basin, they got into the mountains. Though they stopped for only a few minutes at noon they proceeded so carefully that night was coming on by the time they reached the high, broken plateau across which Burnett had led them on the night the dam was destroyed.

They crossed into the Buckskin Hills and turned into higher country. When they found a spring they camped for the night. It was noon of the following day before they located a spot from which, with the aid of the glasses, they could command a broad view of the lower hills. Recalling that Burnett had had no difficulty in showing them the way to upper Black Tail Creek, they were agreed that wherever he and Annette were in the habit of meeting it was not far from that trail. They watched it all afternoon without seeing anyone.

"I wouldn't expect them to be meeting every day," said Hamlin. "We'll have to be patient."

The following afternoon their patience was rewarded when they saw Annette coming from the direction of the T Bar house. She rode openly and without ever glancing back, proof enough that she was not worried about being followed or watched. When she reached a grove of aspens she turned into them and they lost sight of her until she emerged further up the slope. She went on for a few yards and got out of the saddle at the base of a bald-faced cliff, ground-tied her horse

and walked back and forth, her impatience and agitation at having to wait clearly visible through the
glasses.

A quarter of an hour passed before the blond man
from Box Elder joined her. She flew into his arms. He
kissed and embraced her passionately. After a few
minutes they disappeared into a shallow cave at the
base of the cliff.

"Some hanky-panky goin' on down there," Skip
grunted obscenely. "She's just crazy about him, ain't
she?"

Hamlin let it pass without comment. The suspicion
he had entertained for weeks was now an indisputable
fact.

Burnett and Annette were in the cave a long time.
When they came out there was an affectionate, long-
drawn-out parting. She turned back for T Bar and he
could be seen striking out for his ranch.

"You satisfied?" Skip inquired ironically.

"I know all I need to know," Hamlin replied. "I can
put the whole thing together now. She was his girl in
Miles City. For sale, of course. But his girl, Tark comes
along and falls for her, brings her up to Broken Rock
and then marries her. Burnett follows her and buys the
Box Elder spread. She sells the old man the idea that
Burnett would be valuable to him. It gives her an excuse for meeting him two or three times a week."

Roberts nodded. "That's spellin' it out. As you said,
he lost his usefulness when you exposed him as an informer. They must have been terribly disappointed at
gittin' so little out of the robbery."

"No doubt of that," Hamlin responded soberly.
"What they hoped to get was a stake big enough to enable them to get out of the country. I'm going to help

them to do that, Skip. I'm going to buy Burnett's ranch."

The Texan stared at him aghast. "You're goin' to risk all that money? You could be mistaken; they may not make a run for it."

Hamlin shook his head adamantly.

"They'll run. I'd risk that money and a lot more to take the heart out of Jep Tark."

All his bitterness seemed to come to the surface. His eyes were cruel and savage.

"We'll stay in the hills tonight," he went on. "In the morning we'll get down into the basin and head for Box Elder."

Hamlin started for the horses. Skip stopped him.

"Pierce, have you given any thought to how she's goin' to git away from T Bar? If she packs a bag, Tark will—"

"She's too smart to try that!" Hamlin snapped. "She'll take her jewelry and what she's wearing. If one of them makes a mistake it'll be Burnett, not her."

14

Burnett was in the house when Hamlin and Skip rode into his yard. He saw them through the window and recognition sent a cold chill running down his back. He thought he knew why they were there and with fear clutching him his first impulse was to seize a gun and defy them. But he didn't have the rashness to attempt it; even in extremity he knew better than to think he was a match for them. Though he had reason to believe he was in deep trouble he decided that his chances of talking his way out of it were better than shooting his way out of it.

Pulling himself together he opened the door and hailed them. "What can I do for you?" he asked with a spurious indifference. Hamlin was not deceived by it, and wanting to put him at ease, he said:

"Burnett, I'm here for only one reason. I saw your ad in the *Monitor*. If you want to show me the spread I may be interested in buying it."

Burnett was hard put to dissemble his relief.

"I'll be glad to show it to you," said he, "though there isn't much that you haven't seen. I bought thirty-two hundred acres from Drew Oliver when I took over the place, along with the water rights in Box Elder. Counting everything I've got just about three hundred head of stock, most of it young stuff. Do you want to have a look at the house?"

"That won't be necessary. I know it needs some repairs and so does the barn. When I was here a couple of times I looked things over. What I want to see is your stock."

They went out on the range for two hours. It was time wasted as far as Hamlin was concerned; the age and condition of the cattle meant nothing to him, but he felt he had to appear interested and ask the questions that a bona fide purchaser might, to the end that it would quiet any lingering suspicion in Burnett's mind. The latter was completely taken in and secretly congratulated himself on finding a possible buyer. No one else had expressed any interest in taking over the ranch.

"There's considerable range east of the creek," Hamlin pointed out. "Government land, I take it. I suppose you use some of it."

"In the spring. There's fairly good grass all the way into the foothills until late June," Burnett informed him. "If I'd had the money I would have bought it. If a man was in a position to do it this spread could be built up. My west line touches Homer Knox's range. I understand Mrs. Knox would like to sell and move to town."

Hamlin agreed that the possibilities were there. They went back to the house and he got out paper and pencil and did some figuring. Skip looked on with an expressionless face. He knew Hamlin was there to buy the ranch and that the price did not matter particularly.

"You're asking eighteen thousand, Burnett," Hamlin finally got around to saying. "That's high. You'll take less, of course."

"I don't know," the other had the temerity to disagree.

"It depends, I suppose, on how bad you want to sell."

"I'm not going to give the place away, Hamlin."

"I wouldn't expect you to," was the quiet answer. "I'll offer you what I think it's worth. If you want to take sixteen thousand I'll buy it."

He could have had it for fifteen or even less. Burnett hesitated a long time, but only because he didn't want to appear too eager.

"All right," he nodded. "If that's all cash, you got a deal."

"Then suppose you meet me in town at the bank tomorrow at eleven. The bank's attorney can draw up the papers." Hamlin got out his wallet. "I haven't much money on me but here's fifty dollars as a binder. You give me a receipt and we'll be all set." Seemingly as a careless afterthought, he added: "How soon will you be off the place?"

"This is Tuesday; by Saturday will give me time enough."

"You don't have to hurry," Hamlin suggested craftily. "I won't be taking possession that soon."

"We'll make it Saturday," Burnett said positively.

"Good enough. Can your boys run the ranch a day or two?"

"They're all right. I'll tell them you're taking over. Will you be keeping them on?"

"You can tell them they don't have to worry about losing their jobs," said Hamlin. "You settle up with them before you leave. From Saturday on they'll be working for me."

Skip and he got away soon after, striking across the basin for town.

"It wouldn't take us out of our way any to go to Cross Keys," the former volunteered. Hamlin said no.

"I don't want to stop there today. I want to get this business off my mind first. We'll know on Saturday how it works out."

Roberts was thoughtful for a moment. "I wonder why Burnett made it Saturday. He almost insisted on it."

Hamlin gave him a bantering smile. "Smart as you are, you ought to be able to figure that out for yourself. He'll see Annette tomorrow or on Thursday for sure. He'll give her a day to get ready."

"You talk like it was an accomplished fact," the Texan flared back.

"I'm betting sixteen thousand dollars on it."

Hamlin was in the bank, waiting, when Burnett arrived, a few minutes before eleven o'clock. Dan Bradshaw, the bank's attorney, had been summoned. They discussed the terms of the sale with him. He made some notes.

"I'll go back to my office and draw up the papers," he told them. "If you will meet me here at two o'clock for signing, we'll go up to the county clerk then and get the deed transferred."

That was done. Hamlin signed a check for the entire amount in favor of the bank. The mortgage and interest amounted to a little better than eight thousand dollars. When that had been satisfied, the president tendered Burnett the balance.

"I wish you luck on the place." Burnett didn't know whether to offer to shake hands or not. Hamlin was glad that he didn't. He sat there with the bank official and the attorney after the blond man left.

"Mr. Hamlin, I made the appraisal when the bank placed the mortgage on the Box Elder ranch," Brad-

shaw remarked. He was comparatively new in Broken
Rock. "It's worth every dollar you paid for it. I suppose you know what you're going to do with it." He
saw that the other did not understand. "I mean, have
you bought it as an investment or do you intend to stay
with it?"

"If I can turn it at a profit I might be interested.
Otherwise I'll stay with it and see what I can do about
building it up."

"The reason I asked," the attorney explained, "was
because whenever we have a news item here at the
bank we like to pass it on to the *Monitor*. You don't
mind?"

"There's no reason why I should," Hamlin answered. He was, in fact, anxious for Jep Tark to know
he had bought the Box Elder ranch.

The story of the sale appeared on the front page of
the following day's edition. Nowhere was it read with
greater interest than at Cross Keys.

"I wouldn't have thought he'd be interested in a
ranch as small as that," Lockhart said when he finished
the brief item. "Wick Burnett couldn't take a livin' off
the place. Of course he wasn't no stockman; but even a
man who knows his business will find it means hard
scratchin'."

To Carla it meant only that Pierce Hamlin would be
remaining in Yellowstone Basin and her heart beat a
little faster.

In Broken Rock, Lin Bible came looking for Hamlin
a few minutes after the *Monitor* was off the press. He
was somewhat exercised over having been left in the
dark.

"What's the idea you buyin' out Burnett?" he demanded crustily. "When I mentioned it the other day

you said you wasn't interested. What made you change your mind so quick?"

"I won't lie to you, Lin; I had my reasons," Hamlin said apologetically, "but I ain't going to tell you what they are. If you'll just hold your horses for two or three days you'll understand."

"I knew there was a trick in it!" the sheriff snorted. "I only hope you ain't outsmartin' yourself."

"Not this time, Lin. I know what I'm doing. Will you please let it go at that?"

"Only if I have to," the old man grumbled. He pulled up a chair and sat down with Hamlin and Skip. They had been talking a few minutes when a train whistled. The sheriff pulled out his watch.

"Number 17, the westbound local," he announced. "Right on time."

"When is she due?" Hamlin inquired casually.

"4:02—"

"She usually on time?"

"Usually—" The sheriff turned on him irritably. "Say, what's trains got to do with what you're up to? You goin' somewheres?"

Hamlin smiled enigmatically. "I'm not going anywhere—not by train."

After the sheriff left them Hamlin caught Skip grinning to himself. "What's so amusing?" he asked.

"You tellin' Lin you wasn't goin' anywhere by train. Bein' so truthful, you didn't include takin' a trip by hossback. In other words, you won't lie to him but you ain't above deceivin' him."

"I don't know about that," the tall man retorted with an edge of resentment. "Not telling him all I know or what my plans are isn't what I'd call deceiving him."

"Oh, forgit it, Pierce! I didn't think you'd take it seriously. I was just tryin' to git a little rise out of you.

Lin may have the laugh on us at that if Burnett and his
lady friend decide to catch the train here in town while
we're hidin' out at that flag stop."

"They'd never risk leaving from Broken Rock."
Hamlin was positive about it. "I know Tark will go after them. The station agent knows that pair by sight;
the old man would only have to question the agent to
find out what train they took and where they were going. They'll flag the afternoon local on Saturday and
board the train there. We can leave here Saturday
morning and be there in plenty time to pick a spot to
watch them."

With nothing to do but wait, Friday proved to be a
long day for them. The hotel porch provided them with
grandstand seats from which they could observe the life
of the town. It was of only slight interest to them. Shep
Henry, the town marshal, made his rounds and jerked
a nod in their direction as he passed.

"Not even a dog fight to break the monotony this
mornin'," Skip complained.

Before noon, however, Jeptha Tark drove into town
with his foreman. Strahorn was handling the reins. The
old man's head was still bandaged. They turned the
corner and Hamlin surmised correctly that Tark had
come in to see the doctor. A few minutes later Strahorn came back alone and drove down to the depot.
Two T Bar riders with led horses joined him there.

"The new men Tark hired in Miles City last week
must be arrivin' this mornin'," commented Roberts.

It wasn't long before they heard the express from
the west blowing for Broken Rock. With a clanking of
brakes it ground to a stop at the depot, discharged its
passengers and express and continued its flight to the
east. Presently a little cavalcade of T Bar riders, with

Strahorn following in the buggy, came up from the tracks.

"Four new ones," said Hamlin. "That'll put T Bar back to full strength. They look more like cowpunchers than gunmen. He could hardly be hiring them just for the fall work."

"No, he's lookin' ahead further than that. After he's shipped his beef he'll no doubt start movin' down the basin again, just as you predicted."

"That may be his intention right now, Skip, but I don't believe he'll have much fight left in him after to-morrow."

Though it was noon, the T Bar men left town without stopping to eat. It was never Jep Tark's way to waste money on his crew. Strahorn drove back to the doctor's, picked up the master of T Bar and brought him around to the hotel. Doc Squires had removed the bandage from Jep's head.

"The old buzzard looks bad," Roberts commented as he watched him get down from the buggy.

"Shaky, all right," Hamlin agreed. "They're going in for dinner."

Strahorn ignored them as he came up the steps. Tark shot a glance of implacable hatred at them. Roberts looked in through a window.

"The dining room doors are open. Are we goin' in?"

"No, I want to enjoy my dinner," Hamlin said thinly. "We'll wait till they get finished."

They took a turn up the street and finding the sheriff in his office, managed to kill half an hour. When they got back to the hotel, Tark's buggy was gone.

Though they ate leisurely it left them with a long afternoon. When the westbound local whistled, Hamlin got out his watch at once.

"Right on the dot again today, Skip. I hope to God she is tomorrow!"

"What difference does it make if she's runnin' a bit late?" Roberts questioned. "You don't expect Tark to be chasin' 'em, do you?"

"I haven't any reason for thinking so. But I'll feel easier when I know they've gone."

"You don't think it'll be to Miles City?"

"No, any place but there. They know if they're followed that Miles City will be the first place Tark will look. I don't believe they'll even risk Billings; I think they'll go as far as Butte. They may get out of Montana altogether and head for California. Their money won't last long. They'll have to land some place where they can find work."

"*Their* kind of work," Skip observed callously.

"Yeh—"

Without divulging their destination to the barn boss or anyone at the hotel, they slipped out of town just before noon the following day. By two o'clock they had hidden their horses and secreted themselves in the scrub cedars on a hill that commanded a view of the flag stop at Basin. In the other direction, with the aid of the glasses, they could see anything moving over the road for a distance of almost two miles.

"We couldn't do better than this," Hamlin remarked. "We can watch the road a long ways and we're close enough to the railroad to see everything that goes on there."

They had two hours to wait. It made the tediousness of the previous day seem as nothing. Hamlin glanced at his watch repeatedly. The minutes seemed to crawl.

"Pierce, you better git hold of yourself," Roberts advised. "You're as nervous as a cat. We still got a long time to wait. I got a deck of cards in my saddle bag. I'll git 'em and spread a blanket. We'll play some seven up; that'll be better than just sittin' here bitin' our nails."

They tried it, but neither was interested in the game. After a few hands the Texan put the cards away. Hamlin picked up the glasses again. Nothing moved over the long stretch of road that was visible. To the north he had a broad view of the Yellowstone and the ferry. He could see Bat Beauchamp dozing in a chair tilted back against the wall of his cabin. All around him the world was at peace. But he knew none. He flipped a cigarette into shape. Half-smoked, he ground it out. Even tobacco had lost its savor.

Another twenty minutes passed. He took it for granted that Burnett had informed himself as to when the local was due.

"Eighteen minutes to go," he muttered. "They ought to be showing up; no reason why he should be drawing it so fine."

Roberts picked up the glasses. A snort of excitement escaped him immediately.

"They're comin', Pierce! A team and buckboard—a man and a woman on the seat!"

Hamlin snatched the glasses. A low cry of satisfaction burst from him. "You're right! It's the two of them! Everything's working out just as I figured!"

Burnett drove past a few yards below them. There was a strained look on his face and on Annette's too. When they reached the railroad he got down at once and set the hand signal. Coming back to the rig, he stood there talking with her. Both kept glancing back as though fearing pursuit, but from where they were they could not see more than several hundred yards of the road.

Hamlin's attention was fixed on them when Skip thrust the glasses in his hands. "Take a look!" the Texan cried. "That's Tark comin' up the road!"

Hamlin put the glasses on the horseman, only half a mile away, who was raking his big roan with the spurs and holding the animal to a slashing gallop. It was Jep Tark!

"Quick, Skip!" Hamlin flung back over his shoulder as he ran to the horses. "We'll have to stop him!"

15

Stony Aiken, the ex-cowpuncher, crippled and ancient, whose job it was to do the chores and keep the T Bar house reasonably clean, was in the parlor sweeping when a sharp yell of exasperation brought him to the ranch office, where Tark sat at his desk working on the ranch books.

"Stony, do you have to kick up all that dust?" Jep demanded fiercely. "Look at it blowin' in here!"

"I was hurryin' a bit, boss," the old man answered apologetically. "I wanted to git through before the missus got back."

"Gits back?" the master of T Bar took him up with an angry snap. "Where's she gone?"

"Ridin', I reckon, though she wa'n't wearin' her ridin' duds. She was dressed up purty fancy. She went out the back way and got on her hoss. I reckon you was takin' yore after-dinner nap."

"All right!" Jep grunted. "Git out of here and go easy with that broom!"

He went on with his figuring for a few minutes and then suddenly slammed his pen down on the desk. Questions were beginning to leap at him. Why would Annette be dressed up to go riding in the hills? Maybe that wasn't where she was going. But where else?

"To say good-by to Burnett!" He was sure of it and

for a moment he felt relieved. "She knows he's leavin' Box Elder."

Surely that was it. He had always been jealous and suspicious that some younger man might try to take her away from him. He had not thought much about Burnett. The man was weak and getting by on a shoestring. Annette liked money too well to be interested in him. But why had she bothered to get dressed up this afternoon? Her riding habit was expensive, the best in the country. And slipping out the back way while he was asleep! The thought brought him to his feet in a hurry and sent him scurrying upstairs. He knew where she kept her rings and bracelets and the diamond brooch he had given her. They were gone!

Panic ran through Jep Tark. With ghastly clarity he saw through it all. Burnett was leaving the country and she was going with him!

He shouted for his roan to be saddled at once. Strapping on his gunbelt, frenzy overcame him as he waited for the horse to be brought to the door. For a man of his years, just recovering from a serious injury, he called on some hidden source of vitality and raced out of the yard, hatless, his coat tails flapping.

The shortest way to the ranch on Box Elder Creek was to cut across to the Squaw, skirt the Blue Flats and strike straight east. That was the course he took, and though he rode fast, his mind worked even faster. He no longer wondered why Pierce Hamlin had bought the Box Elder ranch; in some way he was in on the secret and he had bought the place to provide Burnett and Annette with the money they needed to get away. He cursed himself for a fool for not having Pierce killed long ago. As for Burnett, he'd settle with him before the afternoon was gone.

Always an arrogant man, prejudiced in his own favor and contemptuous of the rights and merits of others, able to blind himself to whatever he didn't want to believe, however unpleasant, he had refused to regard Pierce Hamlin as anything more than a nuisance. Now suddenly he realized the enormity of his mistake; all his setbacks and agony were traceable to Hamlin. He could hate and despise him, but he could no longer deny the truth.

It was indicative of the deterioration of the man that even with desperation tearing at him he was forced to admit as much.

Though he clipped off every minute he could, it was three o'clock and after when he pulled the roan to a slithering stop in the Box Elder yard. A wild yell brought one of the boys from the barn. His violent, rapid-fire questioning quickly informed him that Burnett had left the ranch some time before by buckboard and that Annette was with him.

"Where was he goin'?"

The young halfbreed shrugged. "He don't say. Go to town, I think."

Tark flashed out of the yard at the reckless haste with which he had arrived. The road was deep in dust. The sharp tracks of the rig were easily followed. When they turned off for the flag stop at Basin he knew what it meant. He had never had any mercy on men or horses. He had none on the big roan now. Far off, he heard the train rattling down the Cherry Hill grade. With a last burst of speed he flashed by the cedars before Hamlin and Roberts got down to the road.

The engineer of the westbound local saw the signal set against him and acknowledged it with a toot of the whistle.

The three-car train was grinding to a stop and Burnett was helping Annette down from the rig when he saw Jep racing toward them, waving his gun, with Hamlin and Roberts a few yards behind and trying desperately to overtake the old man.

The conductor had come down from the nearest coach. Annette screamed as Burnett hurried her toward the steps. Passengers were putting their heads out of the open windows, wondering what was happening. Without a moment's hesitation Tark sent two crashing shots into Burnett. He dropped as though poleaxed. Hamlin flung himself at the old man, knocked the gun out of his hand and pulled him out of the saddle.

Annette, crying hysterically, was on her knees beside Burnett, and so was the conductor. Roberts ran over to them.

"He's still alive, Pierce!" the latter called.

Hamlin's attention remained riveted on Tark. Jep's lined face worked convulsively as he gave way to his insane rage.

"God damn you, Hamlin, you was helpin' them to git away!" he screeched. "That's why you bought his ranch!"

"That's exactly why I bought it," was the stony answer. "I'm glad you know it. I promised you I'd bring you to your knees and I've done it."

"You've done nothin'!" Tark said wildly. "No man's takin' my wife away from me. She's goin' back to T Bar!"

"No! No!" Annette screamed. "I won't go back there with you, you filthy old beast! I hate you and your lousy money. I don't know how I stood you as long as I did!" She appealed to Hamlin. "Don't let him take me back! Please!"

"If she's his wife you better not interfere," the conductor advised. "She won't have to put up with him for long if this man dies."

"I don't intend to interfere, as much as I'd like to," Hamlin said grimly. "If you'll back up your train we'll put this man in the baggage car. I'll go to town with him and get him to a doctor."

Annette tried to get to her feet. Her knees gave way. Roberts caught her as she fainted.

"Put her in the rig, Skip," Hamlin told him. "You get in with her, Tark, and get out of here. That outfit belongs to me. You see that it's returned to Box Elder."

The master of T Bar tied the roan to the end gate and taking his seat in the buckboard drove away rapidly. The train backed up and Burnett was placed on the floor of the baggage car.

"You come in with the horses, Skip," said Hamlin. "I'll see you in town this evening."

Doc Squires said Burnett could not live; that it was only a matter of hours. Broken Rock began to buzz as word of what had happened at Basin went winging over town. Lin Bible arrived at the doctor's a few minutes after Burnett was brought in. Hamlin was there. He gave the sheriff a frank and detailed account of the shooting and what had led to it. Jim Nevins, the district attorney, came then and the story had to be repeated.

"Doc, is there any chance that Burnett will regain consciousness sufficiently to make a statement?" Nevins asked.

Squires shook his head. "I can't say. His pulse is very weak. Since he's in no great pain, I think it would be foolish to probe for the slugs. It's the one under his heart that's causing the trouble; he's bleeding internally."

"Well, if he does come around for a few minutes, you get word to me; I'll be here in a hurry."

He left and Lin and Hamlin sat down on a bench under a tree in the backyard. Some things were now as plain to the sheriff as they were to Jep Tark. Hamlin didn't hold anything back.

"All your schemin' has come to nothin', Pierce." Lin's tone was sober and regretful. "A minute or two more and you'd have got away with it."

"It didn't go the way I expected," Hamlin conceded, equally sober, "but I wouldn't say it was for nothing. Tark can keep Annette a prisoner at T Bar, but he knows he's lost her. He was like a madman, Lin. I don't see how anything can save him if Burnett dies. The law can't hold it a justifiable homicide. Self-defense won't enter into it; Burnett wasn't armed."

Lin Bible nodded. "I won't dispute that. When I said your schemin' had come to nothin' I meant it hadn't come off the way you planned. You wanted to see Jep chasin' that pair to hell and gone and battin' his brains out when he was unable to catch up with him. Without intendin' to you've done worse than that to him; he may hang. I got no sympathy for him. The only one I pity is little Annette. Oh, I know she's bad, but she's a woman, Pierce. God knows what Jep is doin' to her."

"That's my feeling too," Hamlin said tightly. "Can't you do something?"

"Do? What the hell can I do? I can't go to T Bar and take her out of that house without evidence that there's somethin' wrong. If Burnett dies, I'll git out there quick enough."

Skip Roberts reached Broken Rock that evening in time for supper. He was surprised to learn that Burnett was still alive.

"I wouldn't have given him more'n an hour or two.

It's a good thing you grabbed Tark's gun when you did or he'd have killed Annette, Pierce."

"I don't believe it. He'd have killed me, no doubt; but he knew what he was doing; he wouldn't have shot her. He may have done worse than that when he got her home. Nothing would be too cruel for him. I spoke to Lin; he says there's nothing he can do without evidence that she's being mistreated."

In the morning they were called to the district attorney's office and questioned about the shooting. Wick Burnett continued to cling to life. Doc Squires had removed the two slugs and tied up some arteries. It was done out of desperation; he still held out no hope of survival.

The statements Hamlin and Skip gave Nevins disclosed nothing new, but they were in agreement as to the details.

"I had Pat Barnes, the conductor, in early this morning," Nevins told them. "He saw it the same way you men did." He looked across his desk at the sheriff. "We're all set to move in on Tark, Lin, but I think we better wait. There's no danger of the old man trying to run out. If we go ahead now the charge will have to be assault with a deadly weapon, nothing more."

"I'm for waitin'," Lin agreed. "Burnett can't hold on much longer."

To the surprise of everyone the dying man showed some improvement that evening. The following morning he regained consciousness for a few minutes. Before the sheriff or the prosecutor could get there, Burnett had relapsed into a coma.

"He'll go fast now," Doc Squires told them. "He won't last till evening."

At noon Joe Strahorn came pounding into Broken

Rock and went to the Sheriff's office at once. He found Hamlin there with Lin.

"Sheriff, you got to git out to T Bar at once and do somethin' about the boss," he burst out, not trying to conceal his agitation. "I swear to God he's gone stark ravin' mad. The first thing he did after he brought Annette back and dragged her up to her room was to run the cook and old Stony, the swamper, out of the house and lock the doors. He sets upstairs by an open window all day long with a rifle in his hands. You can't git near the house without bein' shot at. I tried it again this mornin'. I figgered if I could talk to him I might be able to do somethin'. When I got about sixty yards of the door he sent a slug whizzin' past my ears."

"What's happened to Annette?" Bible asked.

"I don't know for sure. By the screaming we heard last night he must be usin' a whip on her. He's got her windows boarded up. They ain't had nothin' to eat in a couple of days now."

Lin questioned him until he was satisfied that the T Bar foreman was not exaggerating the seriousness of the situation.

"I've never had a case like this dumped in my lap since I took office," he declared. "I'd like to have Jim Nevins hear what you have to say, Joe." He reached for his hat. "The three of us better walk up to the courthouse."

Strahorn repeated his story to the prosecutor.

"I got no use for that woman," he went on, "but I don't hold with treatin' her that way. Anythin' can happen. I don't want to be blamed for it. That's why I came in."

Nevins turned to the sheriff.

"We can't stall along any further, Lin. We'll have to charge Tark with assault with a deadly weapon and let it go at that for the present. You better swear in some deputies and get out there. After you've taken him into custody, see what you can do for his wife. Whatever you do will be all right with me."

Lin Bible nodded gravely. "If he won't submit to arrest, Jim, I may have to kill him."

"If he resists arrest it will be your duty to kill him. I know you won't be hasty."

They talked for a few minutes. The sheriff got to his feet, Hamlin and Strahorn did likewise. As they were about to leave, Nevins' clerk ran in with the news that Wick Burnett was dead.

"Wal, that puts a different face on it!" Lin exclaimed.

"It does," Nevins agreed. "It's murder now. Don't take any chances with him, Lin."

"Where's Skip?" the sheriff asked as they reached the street.

"At the hotel."

"Git him. The two of you be at my office, ready to ride, in ten minutes. You'll go with us, Joe. We'll stop at Cross Keys and pick up a couple more men."

Before they left town Strahorn got Hamlin aside for a moment. "When I tipped you off to Annette I didn't figger it would end this way. All I wanted to do was git rid of her. When the old man found out, I thought he'd kick her off the ranch. That would have satisfied me."

"You needn't distress yourself over what you told me," Hamlin assured him. "I knew there was something going on between Burnett and her long before you said anything. If we get her out of this mess alive she'll own T Bar when the estate is settled. She may sell it, or if she's got any sense at all she'll put you in charge and spend her time in Miles City or some place where the lights are bright." He gave Strahorn an amused glance. With a quiet, ironic laugh, he said, "That would be a neat little twist, wouldn't it?"

The T Bar foreman shook his head and scowled. "She'd never give me a break like that. She doesn't like me any better than I like her."

"Maybe not, but she knows the kind of a job you've done for the old man; she may figure you'd do the same for her."

At Cross Keys they were acquainted with what had transpired at the lonely flag stop at Basin and that Tark had taken Annette back to T Bar, as everyone in the basin knew by now, but they knew nothing of the situation there or that Wick Burnett was dead. When they saw the sheriff riding in with Hamlin, Skip and Joe Strahorn they sensed at once that something further was amiss.

Lin told them why he was there. Though Carla had had several days in which to adjust herself to the knowledge that the attention Burnett had paid her was just a ruse to divert attention from his affair with Annette her face paled momentarily on learning that he was dead.

"I want to deputize a couple of your men, Tom," said Lin. "If you want to volunteer to go up with us I'd appreciate it. I don't know what I'm goin' to run into. The first thing to do is surround the house. Strahorn says his men will support me. I want to take Jep alive if I can."

"I'll be glad to go," Lockhart replied. "We'll take Buck and Andy with us. They're down the yard. Let's speak to 'em."

Hamlin remained behind when the others left. He felt strangely embarrassed at being alone with Carla.

She betrayed her own tension by saying rather point-lessly:

"You are looking well, Pierce. Would you like to sit down for a minute?"

"Just for a minute."

He had a great deal to tell her, but he didn't know where to begin. There was a witchery about her for him that dried up his thoughts and stilled his tongue. She mentioned Burnett.

"I understand you've admitted that the only reason you bought the Box Elder ranch was to provide him with money for what followed."

"No, that's not true," he contradicted more sharply than he realized. "I bought the place to provide him with money to get out of the country not for what followed. I had no idea it would lead to his death and probably to hers; it was Tark I was striking at. Do you hold it against me, Carla?"

"No, I don't know that I do," she murmured pensively. "He was so worthless and treacherous, but I can't help pitying him a little, and her too. You can't be blamed for what happened at Basin; you couldn't have known it would end that way. I only hope you find her alive and unharmed."

"So do I. I never had any feeling about Annette; I was interested only in pulling Jeptha Tark down."

"I know," she said softly, her voice tight in her throat. "It's been your life since you came back. I hope when it's all over that you'll get the bitterness out of your heart and be able to laugh again."

"I shall—if you'll help me a little, Carla."

Her smile was answer enough. Lin and the others were riding up to the gallery.

"I'll have to go now," he told her. "I'll stop on the way back."

16

The sheriff led Hamlin and the others in a wide circle around the T Bar yard and came up in back of the bunkhouse. Work on the ranch had come to a standstill. Some of the crew lounged about the rear door; some were in their bunks; across the way others were gathered in the barn. It was apparent that no one was needlessly exposing himself to a chance shot from the main house.

The men gathered about the door, until recently at war with the Hamlin and the basin men, regarded the latter coolly. They moved aside to permit Strahorn and Lin to enter. A slug thudded into the front door when the T Bar foreman opened it a few inches.

"His mind may be cracked but there ain't nothin' wrong with his shootin', Lin. He musta seen us ride in."

The sheriff peered through the narrow opening. Tark was down on his knees at one of the open upstairs windows, his rifle resting on the sill.

"Crazy! Plumb crazy!" Bible growled.

He was familiar with the big, ugly house and the ground that surrounded it. For fifty to sixty yards on all four sides it stood out in the open. To approach it by stealth was impossible; a jack rabbit couldn't have found cover out there.

"Where's Annette's room, Joe?"

"Around to the right. You'll see the two windows he's boarded up."

The sheriff closed the door. He and Strahorn rejoined Hamlin and the others

"I'm goin' to stick to my original idea and surround the place. Can you git over to the barn without him seein' you?" he asked the foreman.

"I can ride down and come up behind the corrals."

"Do it. Better take a couple of these men with you, so you'll have enough. You cover the north side and the rear; I'll take the front and south side. When you're in position, pass word to me."

"Lin, you ain't goin' to try to rush the house?" Tom Lockhart questioned.

"No. When I've got him surrounded I'm goin' to walk out and give him a chance to surrender."

"That's being foolhardy!" Hamlin protested hotly. "He'll pick you off. Your badge won't mean anything to him."

"Mebbe not. When I call on him to throw away his gun and he refuses, half a dozen of you start stitchin' holes around the window. That may convince him."

Strahorn and three of his men left at once. Lin disposed his men, leaving it to Hamlin, Skip, Lockhart and the Cross Keys riders to watch the front. Half an hour passed before Strahorn shouted from across the yard that he was ready.

Hamlin and Roberts were down behind a wagon box, their guns trained on the window, when Lin opened the bunkhouse door.

A shot greeted him as he stepped out that carried away his hat. Undeterred, he advanced ten yards.

"Jep, you throw out that rifle and give yourself up!"

he called out. "I'm arrestin' you for the murder of Wick Burnett!"

He could have saved his breath. With a defiant, insane laugh Tark flung his gun to his shoulder. Hamlin and Skip were waiting for such a move. The pattern of their shooting smashed the glass of the upper sash and sent splinters flying from the window frame and sill. Lockhart and his men joined in.

The master of T Bar had sense enough to know that he was safe if he hugged the floor. As soon as the spattering shots ended, he popped up and again flung his rifle to his shoulder and snapped a slug at Lin. The fusillade began anew and Tark dropped out of sight.

The sheriff took cover behind the wagon box.

"It's no use, Lin," Lockhart ground out. "He won't give himself up. Evenin's comin' on; we'll do better if we wait till dark. We can git in the house then without bein' shot up."

"Tom's right," Hamlin spoke up. "Once we get inside we can take him easy enough."

"I ain't waitin' till dark," Lin declared doggedly. "There's better than twenty of us; no one man can hold out against such a bunch."

Before he could say more, shooting broke out from the rear of the house. It drew an angry answer from Strahorn's men. It ended as suddenly as it began and the early evening grew still again.

"We'll put some lead into that house from all sides now," Lin growled. "We'll see what he makes of that."

For twenty minutes a score of guns erupted violently. Not a pane of glass in the T Bar house remained unshattered. The bombardment was noisy, awesome, but seemingly it accomplished nothing. When Lin again called on Jeptha Tark to give himself up, he got no answer.

Strahorn worked around to the sheriff and the group gathered behind the up-ended wagon box. Bible met him with a question.

"You seen anythin' of him since the shootin' stopped?"

"Not a thing. But I got news for you. Annette is alive, at least she was a few minutes ago. I heard her screamin'. I figger the old man knows the jig is up and is gittin' desperate. Crazy as he is he may kill her if we don't git in there right away. If we can reach the back door it won't be no trick to bust in. The back stairs are just inside. I'm willin' to try if you'll keep him busy for a few minutes."

"I'll go with you," Hamlin said without hesitation. "Get a couple of axes, Joe."

Though there were several dozen axes on the ranch Strahorn had to stop to think before he could recollect where to find two. The ranch forge, below the bunkhouse, was the nearest place. He ran that way, zigzagging to avoid a shot from an upper window.

As the others waited they heard a single shot fired within the house. They took it for granted that Jep was sniping again from the rear.

Strahorn was running back with the axes when Tom Lockhart cried: "There's smoke comin' out of the roof! Jep's set the house afire!"

Even as they watched flames broke through the bone-dry shingles and spread rapidly. Hamlin grabbed an axe.

"The fire's in the rear!" he whipped out. "We'll have to go through the front!"

He and Strahorn ran up the steps, smashed the door and kicked it open. Lin and the others poured in after them. They found Jeptha Tark crumbled up in a chair, the position of the body and his rifle leaving no doubt that he had died by his own hand. There wasn't much smoke on the lower floor, but they could see it was bad up above. Skip and Buck Ross picked up the body and carried it into the yard.

Hamlin and the T Bar foreman went up the stairs together. Flames were licking up the south wall. They found Annette's room. Using their axes again they burst through the door. Tark had taken away her clothes and she lay face downward on the bed, unconscious but clutching the little leather bag that held her miserable jewelry, not a stitch on her. Her back was criss-crossed with the welts of the whippings he had given her.

Hamlin wrapped a sheet around her and snatched up a blanket.

"I'll get her out, Joe! See if you can find some clothes for her. You don't want to be long!"

He carried her to the bunkhouse and placed her on a bed. A bucket of water stood near the door. He bathed her face. The cold water began to revive her. Strahorn hurried in with an armful of feminine clothing. The sheriff was with him.

"What shape is she in?" he demanded.

"Her back is cut up; Tark must have given her a terrible beating. I think it's mostly nerves and hunger, Lin."

Bible went over to her. She opened her eyes and recognized him.

"Don't try to talk," he told her. "We'll git to the doctor's as quick as we can." He got Strahorn's attention. "Joe, you have a team hitched to a light wagon. Put some hay in it for her to lay on and start for town. Take the road west of Ten Mile; it's the shortest. I'll go in with you."

The house was burning fiercely by now. There was

water in Black Tail, but with only buckets to fight the fire the effort would have been useless.

"She'll burn to the ground!" Lin rapped. "Pierce, you git some of these T Bar men to help you; find a tarp and roll Jep in it and carry him into the barn. I'll send the undertaker out."

By the time he and Strahorn left, the house was half consumed. Hamlin and the others stood around watching the flames finish their work. He was glad to see it go. It seemed to erase a thousand unhappy memories.

On their way across the basin Lockhart stopped at Alva Williams' and several other ranches to give them the news. It took time and it was black night before they reached Cross Keys. Questions had to be answered. Hamlin left it to Lockhart to do the talking.

Food was Hattie Lockhart's remedy for easing any situation and though it was late, she insisted on going to the kitchen and preparing supper.

"There's no reason, Pierce, why you and Skip should make the long ride to town tonight," said Carla. "You can stay here and go in in the morning."

"Of course they'll stay; we won't take no for an answer," said her father.

"That seems to settle it," Hamlin laughed.

Their conversation as they sat on the gallery centered inevitably on the passing of Jep Tark.

"I suppose if he'd lived he would have been put away for the rest of his life," Carla remarked. "It's better this way—better for everyone."

"I think so," Hamlin agreed. "It closes the book on a lot of things I want to forget. No matter whether T Bar is sold, broken up, or continues as it is, Yellowstone Basin will no longer be an armed camp. For the first time in years there'll be real peace in the basin."

After supper he strolled down to the bridge with Carla. The moon was full and the night was beautiful.

"Now that it's all over I suppose you feel let down and don't know what to do with yourself," she said as they watched Black Tail purling along in the moonlight.

"Oh, I've got some plans," he replied. "I was thinking I might make over the house on Box Elder, inside and out, get rid of the old furniture and have everything new; buy about five thousand acres of Government land east of the creek, and if Mrs. Knox wants to sell, I'd make a deal with her. That would give me a big piece of range. I'd have to stock it. For a couple of years it would be a case of everything going out and nothing coming in. But I could get by; I'll have some money coming from the range I leased to Dallas Wilcox and Price Pickens."

"It sounds very ambitious, Pierce." She looked up at him, her eyes warm and bright. "I've always thought Box Elder was the prettiest spot in the basin."

"And it's not very far from Cross Keys," he said, with a sober smile. "Carla, do you think you could be content there with me? You know I love you. It's you or no one for me. Do you think enough of me to be my wife?"

"Pierce! Oh, Pierce!" she cried happily. "I've been waiting for you to ask me!"

He swept her into his arms and kissed her fondly.

The minutes fled unnoticed as he held her close in his strong arms.

"Are you happy, darling?" he murmured.

"So happy, Pierce!"

"It'll take two or three weeks to get the house ready

for you, Carla. I want you to select everything. If you'll meet me in town this week end you can pick it out, and we can get the license. No need for any waiting about that. If—" He checked himself suddenly. "We'll have to tell your folks. How do you think they'll take it?"

"Suppose we find out," she said, her face aglow. "I'm sure they're still up."

They walked back to the house hand in hand. There was no one on the gallery, but they saw her father in the living room reading his newspaper. Mrs. Lockhart was seated across the room at a small table, sewing by the light of a shaded lamp. Her hands were never still. She looked up as they came in; Tom went on reading. Carla glanced at Pierce.

"Shall I tell them or will you?" she whispered.

"I'd rather it came from you," he answered.

Carla took a deep breath. "Dad, Mother, Pierce has asked me to marry him."

Tom Lockhart tossed his paper on the floor excitedly. "Good heavens, I hope you said yes!"

"I did, Dad—"

Mrs. Lockhart came over and kissed the two of them. Her eyes were bright with tears, but she was pleased.

"I'm not a bit surprised," she said. "Carla is a very determined girl, Pierce. I knew she'd never let you get away."

Hamlin backed off with mock chagrin. "Do you mean to say she's had her cap set for me all this time?"

"Why, of course!" Mrs. Lockhart said teasingly. "You've got a lot to learn about young women, Pierce. They do the marrying, not the men."

It was a happy moment for all four. Pierce spoke

about his plans for repairing and refurbishing the Box Elder house.

"It'll take two to three weeks."

"That'll work out fine," Lockhart told him. "I'll have my beef shipped by then. We'll have a big wedding. We'll have everybody in the basin here."

When Hamlin left for the bunkhouse, Carla stepped out on the gallery with him and kissed him good night.

"I'm so happy and excited I know I shan't sleep a wink," she murmured as he held her close.

Doc Squires permitted Annette to leave her bed to attend the brief services for Wick Burnett. Joe Strahorn drove to the cemetery with her. Jep Tark was buried the same afternoon. His lawyer and the president of the bank were the only "mourners."

Hamlin met Strahorn on the street later in the afternoon. He had come to have an obscure liking for the man.

"I'm glad to see that Annette is recovering," he said. "Have you come to an understanding with her?"

"I think it's goin' to work out all right for me. I'm goin' to make the gather and attend to the shippin'. If she gits T Bar she says she wants me to run it for her. Seems she's got relatives in Sioux City. She's goin' back there when things are settled. She ain't so bad when you git to know her."

Hamlin could not help thinking that Strahorn's self-interest had something to do with his changed opinion of Annette.

"It's nice things are going your way, Joe. I understand you've fired the gunmen Tark brought up."

"That's right. I ain't payin' no man wages just for packin' a gun. I'm goin' to run that spread for her so there won't be a dollar wasted. If the folks in the basin play fair with me I'll shoot square with them."

Seated in the sheriff's office that evening Hamlin acquainted Lin with what Strahorn had had to say.

"That's all to the good, Pierce. He'll do about as he says. I saw Skip before he left for Box Elder this mornin' with George Anderson."

"Did he tell you he's agreed to stick with me and ramrod the spread?"

"Shucks, I took that for granted. Anderson is a good builder. He'll put that house in shape and won't overcharge you. When you were buyin' range east of the crick, why didn't you buy all of it?"

"Money," Hamlin said laconically. "I don't want to spread myself too thin; it's going to take a few thousand dollars to stock that place properly. Speaking of money, Lin, what's going to be done with the money Burnett had on him?"

"It'll be turned over to the public administrator and held in escrow till somebody shows up to establish a claim to it. Burnett had relatives back in Kentucky. They'll be heard from."

Carla arrived in town with her father early Saturday morning. She was radiant in her excitement. Hamlin was proud of her as they stepped into Grassel and Kuhn's big store and Herman Grassel, the firm's senior partner, showed them through the furniture department. Some of the things she wanted had to be ordered from catalogues. The old German assured them that he would have the rugs and half a dozen other items in Broken Rock in two weeks.

"We're spending too much money, Pierce," she protested when he told Grassel to include a mahogany table that she admired.

"We won't be doing this again, Carla. I want you to have the best."

The morning was gone before they were finished. Walking back to the hotel to have dinner with her father, he said:

"I wonder if the two of us could go out to the cemetery to my mother's grave this afternoon."

"I'd be happy to go, Pierce. It's impossible to buy any flowers in Broken Rock, but I'm sure I can get a bouquet from Mrs. Nevins' garden."

They drove out early in the afternoon. Carla knelt down at the grave to place her bouquet. Hamlin got down with her and they knelt there in silence for some minutes.

"I'm never going to speak of this again, Carla," he said humbly, "but I want you to understand that it was what Jep Tark did to her that made me hate him; it wasn't what he did to me. A debt like that can never be squared, I know. I did my best to make him pay. I hope she knows and understands."

"I'm sure she does, Pierce."

"Then we can leave; we've got our life together ahead of us."